You Belong With Me

You Belong With Me

SHUCHI BATRA

NU VOICE
PRESS

First published by NU VOICE PRESS 2024
An imprint of Hubhawks Pvt. Ltd
www.nuvoicepress.com

This is a work of fiction. Space and time have been rearranged to suit the convenience of the book. Except for public figures, hotels, and institution names, any resemblance to persons living or dead or the real events are purely coincidental. The opinions expressed in the book are those of the characters, and should not be confused with that of the Author.

ISBN: 978-81-966888-2-0

Typeset by Saanvi Graphics, Noida
Printed at Thomson Press
Published by Nu Voice Press

For my husband, Manoj,
My mother, Vandana,
My in-laws, Gokulavalsan and Prasanna,
My uncle, Pankaj and aunt, Sangeeta,
My sisters, Sugandha and Vrinda,
My best friends, Deepika, Alaa, and Seema, and
My Instagram family.

Preface

This tale of love and heartbreak is centred around my best friend, Siddhartha, also known as Sid. Sid's heart got shattered in the past, leaving him broken and lost in a maze of sadness. The wounds of his past love, Siya, ran deep. For two long years, he struggled to find his way back to the light, trying to fix the fragments of his soul.

During the journey of self-healing, fate played its part, and Sid met a woman named Alia. Hailing from the enchanting land of Jordan, Alia possessed a magnetic allure. On their first ever encounter, Alia casted a spell over Sid, reigniting a flame that he believed to have lost forever...

Alia saw through the walls that Sid had built around his heart. As the days turned into nights, Sid found refuge in a secret diary. He yearned for Alia, who had captivated his heart and soul. Each word carried the weight of his vulnerability, and every page overflowed with raw, unfiltered emotions.

However, Sid could not deliver his diary to Alia. So, he trusted me with his heart's secrets, and, I became his messenger. But there was more to this delivery, and I will reveal that at the end of the story.

After knowing Sid's story, I could feel the intensity of his emotions. It was not an ordinary love, but a romance blooming from the pieces of a broken heart. Sid's love for Alia was a ray of hope, bravely facing the shadows of the past and aiming for a brighter future.

Dear reader, brace yourself for what comes next. This was just a glimpse. Await a bookish journey that will tug at your heartstrings, from the beginning until the very end.

Get swept away into a world full of drama, love, and emotions!

The Present

I want a second chance with you
in a world
where
time is infinite
boundaries will not divide
religion will not win
and loving you is not a sin.

1

Two days before the flight.

Dear diary,

My heart was pounding with nervousness and anticipation as I stood outside Alia's door, clutching the diary and a letter in my hands.

Taking a deep breath, I knocked softly on the door. Moments later, it swung open, and there stood Alia. She looked beautiful and radiant as ever, but there was a fire in her eyes that I had never seen before. I could tell that she was angry, and I braced myself for the storm that was about to hit me.

I have never seen Alia this way. There was a sadness in her presence. The sadness that I was responsible for. The sadness that shattered my heart into a million pieces, because I knew that I could never erase it. Alia's hair was falling on her face, and I wanted to push them back like always, but I knew that I had lost the right to touch her ever again. She was wearing a red dress that made her blue eyes pop, and even while angry, she looked beautiful.

"What do you want?" she snapped.

"I... I brought this for you," I stammered, extending the diary towards her.

Her eyes fell on the diary, and I saw hurt and anger flush in her gaze. "So, you've come to say goodbye," she said coldly.

"I... I did not want to leave without giving this to you," I replied, my voice barely audible.

"Well, congratulations. You got what you wanted," she retorted, snatching the diary and the letter from my hands and throwing them away.

"I never wanted to hurt you, Alia. You must believe me," I pleaded, my heart breaking at seeing the pain in her eyes.

"You've already hurt me enough," she said, her voice trembling. "You promised me a forever, but all I got was a goodbye."

"I'm so sorry, Alia. I never wanted to leave you."

"If you loved me, you would have stayed and fought for us."

"I did fight, Alia. But sometimes love is not enough. We both know that," I said, trying to maintain my composure.

She turned away, unable to look at me any longer. "Just go, Siddhartha. Go and live your dream. That is all that matters now," she said, her voice barely above a whisper.

I wanted to reach out and hold her, tell her that she was still my dream. But, I knew that it would only make things worse. So, with a sinking heart, I walked away, leaving Alia standing at that doorstep.

I knew that I had exited with broken hearts and shattered dreams. I knew that our love story had ended. But a part of me still held on to that faint hope. The hope that maybe someday, our paths would cross again, and we would find our way back to each other.

I had to let go and move on, with the memories of our love and the pain of an unfinished goodbye in my heart. At least for now.

Love,
Siddhartha.

2

The day of the flight.

Me: Hi, Alia. I am at the airport. I wanted to give you the diary and a letter the other day, but you did not accept. I am unsure if you will reply to this, but I could not stop myself from sending a last message before I leave.

Alia: Hi, Siddhartha. I wish you a happy journey. Please do not message me from now on.

Me: I miss you, Alia.

Alia: Ok.

Me: You do not miss me at all.

Alia: You did not do anything to make me miss you. You just left me for your dreams.

Me: It's not like that. Trust me.

Alia: Ok, enough. I can only go in circles occasionally. You wanted to go, and you left. Now, what do you want from me?

Me: Nothing. Have a great life. But, always remember that I love you.

Alia: I don't know if I can ever believe in those words coming from your mouth. But I do know what I want to say to you.

Me: What?

Alia: Go to hell. Just go to hell.

Me: Maybe I will.

3

Room Operator: Hello, Ms. Alia. Someone named Aditya is here waiting for you. Can you please come to the reception?

Alia: Who is Aditya? I don't know anyone by that name.

Room Operator: Aditya says that he is Mr. Siddhartha's friend and wants to deliver something to you urgently.

Suddenly, a bell rang in Alia's mind. Aditya was Siddhartha's only friend, other than herself. They had known each other since their childhood, and Aditya had been pivotal in shaping Siddhartha's life. Siddhartha considered Aditya as family, so he was both his brother and best friend. They had shared life's highs and lows together. Alia remembered that Siddhartha had shown her Aditya's picture once, during a conversation about his life.

Alia: Hmm, I will be down in 5 minutes.

During this time, all Aditya could think about was, how difficult it must have been for Siddhartha to leave his love behind and chase his dreams. He did not know how to confront Alia and what to say. He was so lost in his thoughts that he did not realise Alia had been saying hello to him. He was abruptly drawn into the real world by Alia's loud voice.

"Hey, Aditya. What are you doing here? What do you want to give me? If it is that stupid diary and the letter, please leave now. I do not want anything," Alia said authoritatively.

"Sid had come two days back to deliver these things to you, but you did not accept. He came straight to my house after that, feeling dejected. He took a promise from me to deliver these to you..."

"I've already told him this, and I am also telling you now... I do not want these stupid things. Go away, or I will call the police!"

"Sid has taken a promise from me. He also messaged me from the airport to deliver these to you as soon as possible. Please accept the letter and the diary. And once you've read them, please call me. There is something that I have to tell you."

"Why did he take a promise from you? What is this game that Siddhartha is playing? If he really loved me, he would have been here himself!" said Alia, snatching the diary and the letter from Aditya's hands and storming towards her room.

Aditya only hoped that Alia would read the diary and give him a call. He was waiting to tell her the truth that was eating him alive. Alia did not know what was about to come into her life. There was a silence before the storm.

Many questions ran through Alia's mind. She eventually decided to read the diary and letter to uncover the truth. She opened the letter first.

Dear Alia,

From strangers
to
till death do us part
we are yet again
back to strangers
but this time
a million miles apart.

I am not sure if these words will ever reach your eyes, but if they have, it means one of two possibilities has come true. Perhaps we are now bound by the sacred vows of marriage, and I am sharing this intimate account with you on the first day of our union. Or perhaps fate had other plans, and we never made it to the end, but somehow this diary found its way into your hands. Regardless of how you came to hold these pages, know that my love for you is boundless, and it will endure through time.

In these entries of my diary, I will narrate how I fell in love with you, and how you captivated my heart like no other. From the very first time that our eyes met, a spark ignited in me, and it only grew brighter with each passing day. Your smile, your laughter, and the way your eyes used to light up when we were together—these moments have etched themselves into my soul.

I don't know what the future holds for us, but what I do know is that my heart is yours, now and forever. You are the one who fills up my thoughts, the one that I dream of at night, and the one whose presence lights up my world.

Whether you hold this diary as a celebration of our love or as a painful reminder of what could have been—I want you to know that I love you deeply and completely. You complete me, and make every moment worth living. No matter where life takes us, remember that you have my heart, and it will always beat for you.

In another life, we will find each other again. Until then, you will reside just beneath my skin. And I will cherish you forever.

Yours,
Siddhartha.

In the Past

Siddhartha

3rd Feb, 2021

Dear diary,

Today marks the beginning of a new adventure, a fresh page, and a new version of myself in life. I will embrace the unknown with joy and bravery, with my head high and my heart full of hope. I feel so alive. I want to pursue everything that I can and should achieve.

You may not know this, but I spent an entire year mourning over what happened to me, and wondering why it happened to me. I created a complex web of thoughts to determine what went wrong and why it did. Was it my fault, or was it just my destiny? Anyway, this is my first diary entry, and I do not want it to be gloomy. So here, I promise to reclaim my life and accomplish everything possible.

And I know that you'll be by my side, at every step, witnessing the journey of a lifetime.

Love,
Siddhartha.

8th Feb, 2021

Dear diary,

It has been a while since I wrote anything. You are my new friend, but I used to have someone like you when I was a child. I would confide everything that troubled me, and he would listen patiently. I don't know what happened, maybe he got lost or thrown away. But I missed him so much that I decided to buy you and start a new chapter in my life.

You see, I have a lot of things to tell you. These are the things that I can't share with anyone else. Things that make me happy, sad, angry, or confused. Things that make me who I am. And one of those things is my love for poetry.

I have been writing poems since I was eight years old. I know it sounds unbelievable, but it is true. One day, I felt a surge of emotions in my mind, so I grabbed a pen and paper and let the words flow. It was like magic, like a gift from the heavens. I felt alive and free.

My first poems could have been better, of course. They were mostly rhymes without much meaning. But as I grew older, I learned to express myself better by crafting more complex and beautiful poems. Poems that reflected my thoughts and feelings, my dreams and fears, my joys and sorrows.

And now, you are the lucky one who gets to read them. You are the new witness in my life and the keeper of my secrets.

And I hope that you will be a good friend to me, as I will be to you.

But before we get into it, let me tell you a little about myself. I was born in Delhi, India. But I did not live there. I lived in a small town called Faridabad, near Delhi. That is where most of my childhood memories are from. And most of them are not very pleasant.

You see, my family was not incredibly happy. My father and my grandmother were always mean to me and my mother. They would yell at us and make us feel worthless. The only person who loved me unconditionally was my mother. She was my angel, my hero, and my best friend.

My parents had an arranged marriage, but I did not know then that my father hated my mother's family and consistently had problems with them. He was also significantly influenced by his mother, who always found faults in everything he did. My mother was a teacher in a government school in Delhi. She took a bus daily from our town to her school, which took one and a half hours each way. I always wondered why my mother had to work when my friends' mothers stayed home and looked after them.

Sometimes, when my father and my grandmother would fight with my mother, I would run to the small prayer room that we had and prayed to God to make them stop. Sometimes, I would fall asleep there and wake up the following day, hoping everything would be better. But it never was.

I don't remember my father ever being lovely to me. He never taught me anything, played with me, or hugged me. He was always angry or absent. I still remember the night he got extremely sick. It was December 3rd, 1996. I was eight years old.

I was sleeping when my mother woke me up. She told me to dress quickly and follow her to the neighbour's house. It was around 3 a.m., and it was freezing and dark outside. I was scared, but I obeyed my mother. She held my hand, and we ran to the doctor's house.

She made me climb over the fence and knock on the door. I looked at her face and saw fear and panic in her eyes. She was sweating and trembling. I did not know what was happening but I did what she told me. After a few minutes, the doctor came out. He looked sleepy and annoyed, but he changed his expression when he saw my mother. He went back inside and came out with a bag. He told us to follow him to our house. We did as he said.

When we got home, he went to my grandmother's room, where my father was lying on the bed. He was groaning and writhing in pain. I did not know what was wrong with him. I thought maybe he had eaten something wrong or had a bad dream. But I was too young to understand.

The doctor gave him an injection and told my mother to take him to a big hospital in Delhi called AIIMS. It was far away but he said that it was urgent. My mother called my aunt, who had a car and asked her to come and help. I asked my mother what was happening, and she told me to go back to sleep. I was sleepy but also curious. But I listened to my mother and went back to my room.

I do not know what happened after, as I was fast asleep, untouched by the drama around me. I was slept peacefully until I heard someone coming into my room.

I have to stop here as it is getting extremely late, and I need to go to the office tomorrow morning. I will tell you what happened in my next entry.

Till then,
Siddhartha.

9th Feb, 2021

Dear diary,

I had to stop writing yesterday because it was past my bedtime, and I was feeling sleepy. But I have so much more to tell you, so let me continue from where I left off.

You see, on that night my grandmother was not at home. She had gone to a wedding in Jammu with her daughter, a state that was far away from ours. My cousin came into my room the following day and shook me awake. She was eight years older than me, and I adored her. She was the daughter of my father's sister, who had gone to AIIMS with my parents. As soon as I opened my eyes, I hugged her and asked where my mother was. I could not see her anywhere in the house. She did not give me a straight answer, but told me that my father was sick, and they had taken him to the hospital. I believed her but wanted to know when my mother would return. I missed her so much. I did not care about my father at all. He was always mean to me and my mother. He was hardly home, and when he was, he sat with my grandmother and talked badly about my mother and her family.

Every morning, when I woke up, my mother would be gone. She left the house by six. My grandmother got me ready for school. That was the only thing she did for me. When I returned from school, my mother would not be home yet. I would sit on the stairs of the veranda and wait for her. When I saw her walking down the street, I would run and hug her. Then, I would follow her to the kitchen, where she would make lunch for my grandmother, herself, and me. My father primarily stayed out of town, as he worked in Marketing.

After lunch, my mother and I would go to our room and nap. Our room was relatively small, but it had everything we needed —a bed, a cooler, a tube light, and a fan. It also had a small prayer room inside, where I would hide when my parents fought. I still remember how we would lie on our beds and share stories of our day. My mother would tell me what happened in her school.

I remember, one afternoon, she told me a funny story about how the bus conductor called her *"Behenji"*. I had never heard that word before, and when I did for the first time, I burst out laughing. I remember how my mother also laughed with me. She hardly ever laughed in that house because of the toxic environment created by my father and his mother. But she laughed with me that day, and I felt so happy. What else does a child want other than his mother's smile?

She used to wear traditional suits at home and sarees when she went to work. She did not have many clothes, she used to wear the same ones repeatedly. Oh, I forgot to tell you, she was a teacher and earned well, but my grandmother took away all her salary. My mother was so obedient that she never complained. She would get some money with which she had to manage our expenses. My mother was not wealthy, but there was not a day when I slept hungry. She used to save all her money for my education and other expenses. My father never shelled out any money on me, so I started developing hatred against him.

I did not have any friends in that small town. Maybe I was too broken inside, even at a young age. I felt unworthy, diary.

I thought that it was worthless to have anyone around me, worthless to have a friend, and worthless to be loved by anyone other than my mother. Because, if my father could not love me, how could anyone else? This feeling stayed with me even when I grew up. I developed issues with abandonment, sadness, and hopelessness.

But let me get back to the story, diary. That day, my cousin came to our house and packed my bag. She took me to her house, where I stayed for two weeks while my father was in the hospital. On the third day, I cried a lot. I wanted to see my mother. I did not care about anyone else, but my mother. I made such a fuss that my aunt and uncle decided to take me to AIIMS, where my parents were. You know, diary, I still remember that evening when I walked into the hospital and saw my mother. I ran to her and hugged her tight. She looked so tired. She looked as if she had not slept for days. She took me to the ICU, where my father was. I did not know what an ICU was, but I thought it was where they kept the sick people. My grandmother was also there, with my mother. She was apprehensive about her son.

My mother held my hand and led me to the ICU. And suddenly, I saw so many people lying on beds, with wires and machines attached to them. They looked sad and in pain. I did not like seeing them, so I just followed my mother. And then I saw a face that I recognised. It was my father, lying on a bed with a white sheet over him. He looked so weak, diary. I had never seen him like that before. He looked at me, and I saw something in his eyes. Something I had never seen before. He looked at me as if he were seeing me for the first time. He called me to come closer, but I was scared. I was scared because he had never shown any emotion towards me in my whole life. And now he was looking at me with such intensity that I did not know what to do. But I still went and sat next to him on the bed.

He held my hand and kept looking at me. He looked at me with love, diary. Love that I had never seen in his eyes before. He wanted to say something, but he did not. Maybe he could not because we had never even talked before. Maybe he was afraid because he was extremely sick. Maybe he was sorry because he had never loved me or my mother. Maybe he realised that he had wasted a lot of time and now did not have much left.

My mother did not say anything, and there was silence in the room. But that day, my father said a lot without even saying a word. And for the first time, I felt like had a father. And I felt happy. I was delighted that he had finally noticed me. I felt a connection with him, and I prayed to God to make him better. But after ten minutes, my aunt came to the ICU and told my mother that it was time to go.

When I heard that, I started crying. Crying, because I did not want to leave my mother. I hugged her and begged to take me with her. But she lifted me and kissed me on the cheek. She told me to be a brave boy and go back home. She promised that she would return very soon, and we would all be together. With tears in my eyes, I kissed my mother back and went to my aunt so we could go back to her house. We had not come in a car but on a scooter. I hopped in between my uncle, who was driving the two-wheeler, and aunty who was sitting behind. It was an uncomfortable journey because I was sitting in whatever little space that I had. I fell asleep thinking about my mother and making plans to see her soon.

We were finally together after two weeks, and it was a happy reunion with my mother. I thought life would become good as I had sensed love in my father's eyes, but the following years were tougher as my father was always sick. The thought alone brings so much pain, and I do not think I can write anymore.

I am sorry, diary. But I will tell you the rest of the story some other time. I am off to bed now.

Love,
Siddhartha.

10th Feb, 2021

Dear diary,

The silence in my room weighs heavy, each tick of the clock reminding me of the gaping void in my life. I have made a pact with myself to fill this void, by sharing my story with you—a stranger, who ironically, feels more familiar than the emptiness around me.

My mother's love had always been a haven, a constant in a world of flux. But then she came, Siya, with her sun-kissed face and a laughter that echoed through my college halls. She became my solace, a love that surpassed even my mother's.

It was the first year of college, the year was 2013. A sea of unfamiliar faces swirled around me, a nervous first-year student in the new city of Jaipur. And then, amidst the chaos, I saw her. Like a ray of sunshine in a sea of grey. Her yellow top and vibrant energy drew me in and she realised that I was watching her.

Siya. Her name was as beautiful as she was. We became friends, confidantes, and then lovers. It was our first love—a whirlwind of stolen glances, whispered secrets, and dreams shared under the starlit sky. With the unwavering faith of youth, I believed that she was my soulmate. But fate had a different script in mind.

After four years of love and laughter, I crumbled to dust in the face of a heart-wrenching truth. I lost a piece of me that day, and

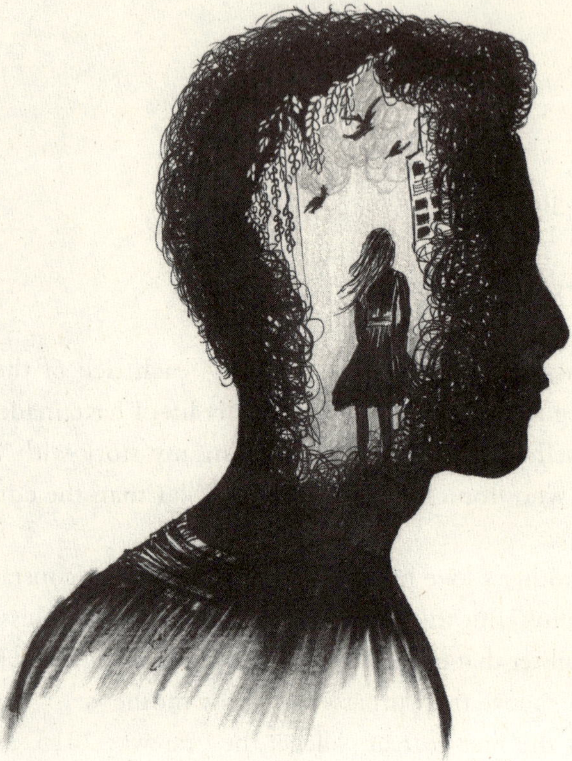

I have not found it since. I wander through life, searching for the lost fragment of my soul in the crowds, but it remains elusive.

Today, I saw her picture on Instagram. It was a snapshot of her happiness, a stark contrast to the darkness that still lingers within me. I questioned everything—our love, her sincerity, even the very nature of time and change. Was it all a lie? Do people just shed their past like old skin, leaving remnants of who they were once?

I deleted the app, the source of my pain, and vowed to never return. This is not the end of my story, but the beginning of a new chapter. A chapter in which I will reclaim myself, where I will focus on healing and building a life that is mine, and not defined by the past.

Will I be able to emerge from this darkness? I do not know. But for now, I will hold onto the hope and write my happy ending.

Love,
Siddhartha.

12th Feb, 2021

Dear diary,

I finished my Engineering in 2017, after which I came back to Delhi. I lived in the shadows of heartbreak for an entire year, trying to make sense of what went wrong. I questioned myself endlessly, wondering if I missed any signs or red flags. I felt like my trust had been betrayed, and I did not know if I could ever open my heart again. It was difficult for me to stay back in India. Wherever I went, I was reminded of Siya. I was also trying to move out, but did not know where to go. Then I remembered my best friend, Aditya. As fate would have it, he referred me to his previous organisation in Dubai. I accepted a job to manage the portfolio for credit cards in a local bank. Aditya helped me so much in coming out of the darkness. He helped me settle in Dubai, and for the last three years, I have called Dubai my home.

Diary, I must confess that I have set my sights on an audacious goal—to study at one of the finest business schools in the United States. The idea of treading the hallowed halls of knowledge, engaging with brilliant minds, and unravelling the intricacies of business and leadership fills me with exhilaration. This dream, once hidden in the shadows of uncertainty, has grown into a steadfast flame that illuminates my path ahead.

Heartbreak, as strange as it may seem, has been a silent ally in forging this resolution. In its wake, I found the strength to rediscover myself, dusting the fragments of my shattered heart, and channelling my energy into something that transcends the mere existence. It forced me to reckon with my limitations and, in doing so, unveiled my potential.

As time passed by, I slowly began to heal. I surrounded myself with friends and family who showed me love and support. They reminded me I was worth more than someone's betrayal. I rediscovered my passions, delved into my hobbies and interests, and found solace in the little joys of life.

While the pain may never disappear entirely, I learned that scars can also be a reminder of strength. I embraced my vulnerability and allowed myself to feel, grieve, and heal. I realised that my worth really did not depend on someone else's actions, and I deserved love and happiness as much as anyone else.

Love,
Siddhartha.

Just because you were my first love
does not mean you would be my last
as I grew older, I realised that
it was just a strong feeling at one time
and now it has sadly passed.

15th Feb, 2021

Dear diary,

Dubai. A city of contrasts, where towering skyscrapers pierce the sky, and ancient souls whisper stories of ages past. I thrive on its diverse flavours, each a delicious bite in the tapestry of my life. My days here are a dance between ambition and the comforting rhythm of daily routines.

Downtown Dubai pulsates with a vibrant energy. It is like walking through a miniature New York City, skyscrapers reaching for the heavens and dreams echoing in their shadows. But when I long for the familiar, a stroll through Old Dubai transports me to Chandni Chowk's bustling streets, spices filling up the air.

My bank, nestled in the heart of Oud Metha, possesses an undeniable Arabic charm. It is a hive of activity, especially during the wee hours, when bankers huddle around the honey of opportunity like bees. Every day, I join their ranks, each striving to build a better tomorrow in this tax-free haven.

My office stands sentinel at the end of the main road, like a silent observer as I navigate the morning chaos. Across the street lies a community garden, a haven of green amidst the concrete jungle. I often see residents there, their faces etched with the quiet determination of everyday life. Tiny Indian restaurants pepper the area, their familiar smells comfort my soul.

Finding a parking spot is a daily battle. While the senior leadership team enjoys the luxury of dedicated spots, I join the rest of the managers in a parking war. Sometimes, luck smiles upon me, but often, I find myself trekking for seven to eight minutes under the Dubai sun. This walk, however, offers a chance to bond with my colleagues. We gather near the entrance, sharing stories and dreams over steaming cups of tea, a moment of respite in the whirlwind.

Initially, I dreamt of an expensive apartment in the European districts. But reality check? My current salary does not allow me to live that dream. So, I have opted for a spacious oasis in the suburbs, a serene escape from the city's clamour.

However, my ambition whispered of bigger things. The corporate ladder beckoned, and an MBA seemed like the key to unlocking its higher rungs. However, pursuing it in India was not an option. My eyes were set on the West, towards the prestigious B-schools in the USA. Last month, I ventured into Old Dubai, the scent of ancient parchment guiding me toward a treasure trove of GMAT books. With a daunting target of 750 out of 800 marks, this international exam stood between me and my dream.

Ten days ago, I traded my suburban oasis for a more strategic location—the Rove Hotel, right across from my office. It is not in the lap of luxury but offers me some precious minutes that I desperately need for my GMAT preparation. My days are a blur of work, study, and snatched moments of sleep. The pressure is immense and a constant companion, but I refuse to let it break me.

I left work at 6 p.m., the city's roar fading as I entered my temporary haven. A cold shower jolted me awake, preparing me for the mental marathon. My room initially served as my battleground, but the unforgiving chair soon became my enemy, giving me a relentless backache. Driven by discomfort, I ventured onto the hotel's rooftop terrace, a hidden sanctuary bathed in moonlight. Here, amidst the murmurs of the city, I found my sanctuary. A lone table became my study haven, my weapons of choice became the GMAT books and a thirst for knowledge.

From 7 to 11 p.m., I waged a war against the test, conquering concepts and strategies. The silence is not absolute, but the distant hums are mere background noise in the symphony of my ambition. A 24/7 shop offered sustenance in the form of protein bars and energy drinks, fuelling my journey.

I have found a newfound sense of purpose one week into my rooftop routine. The solitude is not isolating, but empowering. I know that someone is always nearby, and that is a comforting thought in the face of a daunting challenge.

This is my story, a testament to the hustle of a banker driven by his dreams. This is Dubai, a city where ambition dances with reality, and I, Sid, will strive to write my own success story.

Love,
Siddhartha.

16th Feb, 2021

Dear diary,

Now, let me share the most unexpected twist that has occurred in my daily routine. Yesterday, while studying on the rooftop terrace, I heard a girl's voice. She was inquiring about the rooftop's hours from the security guard. Curious, I turned around, and the moment my eyes met hers, I felt a strange sense of familiarity. It was bewildering because I had never seen her before, but she felt like someone I had known for ages.

Where do I start?
I looked at her once,
knowing that I wanted her forever
as if she was in my heart across all my lifetimes.

I could not find any words; her presence had transfixed me. She had an aura that captivated me, even though I could not understand why. Maybe our paths had crossed in a previous life or in some parallel universe. I kept gazing at her, trying to unravel the mystery of this inexplicable connection.

I know you
from some other life
because how else can you explain
this feeling otherwise?

But reality kicked in, and I had to return to my studies. Nevertheless, the memory of that moment still lingers in my mind, leaving me with a melancholy ache. One day, I will get to know her and discover why she felt so familiar. Until then, I will keep pushing forward, focusing on my dreams, and hoping fate has something extraordinary in store for both of us.

Love,
Siddhartha.

Two hearts
that intuitively know
and make a promise to never let go.

18th Feb, 2021

Dear diary,

You will not believe the array of emotions that I have been experiencing lately. Remember the girl that I had mentioned earlier, the one I saw on the rooftop a few days back? Well, she has been on my mind ever since then. I cannot shake the feeling that we have some mysterious connection, as if we have known each other in some other time or dimension.

I have heard of 'the red thread'—a mystical thread that binds two souls destined to meet and know each other across different lifetimes. I cannot help but wonder if this is what I am experiencing with her. It is almost as if the universe conspired to bring us together, and that there is something significant between us.

She comes to the rooftop daily, and last night, fate led her to sit in front of my table. I could not help stealing glances at her. She exuded an air of mystery and intrigue, like a flickering flame in the darkness. I also sensed a deep sadness in her eyes, a pain that seemed to echo in my heart. I felt an urge to comfort her, hold her close, and tell her that everything would be all right.

She looked at the stars, the comets, and the moon, and I stared at her.

But I could not gather the courage to approach her. She seemed lost in her thoughts, desperately trying to quit smoking, and I did not want to intrude. Instead, I was drawn to her from a distance, mesmerised by her enigma.

As the evening went on, I kept stealing glances at her, unable to resist the pull of this unexplainable connection. The universe was playing a cosmic symphony, orchestrating our intertwining paths. Yet, I did not dare make a move, unsure if she would welcome my presence. A couple of times, I realised that she was looking at me too, and whenever I noticed, she looked away.

A flashback to when I initially met Siya came crashing into my mind. I remembered how Siya and I would steal glances in the crowded areas. And I still remember how excited I would feel all day if I found her looking at me. I also remember approaching Siya and beginning a friendship, which took me one whole month. I was so shy back in college. I still am, but I am a little better than my younger self.

Suddenly, she looked at me and smiled, and an overwhelming desire to talk to her consumed me. But the memories of my past came crashing down, reminding me of the emotional turmoil that I had fought so hard to overcome. I could not bear being dragged back into that abyss again. Was I suddenly missing Siya? What if I thought I had moved on, but honestly, my heart still yearned for her?

I thought I had moved on, and still,
I cannot meet someone new
because whenever I try to, my heart
oh, my stupid heart takes me back to you.

As I stood up to leave, our eyes met for a fleeting moment. She smiled at me, her eyes beckoning me to come closer, and unravel the stories hidden within. But I resisted. I said a simple "hi" and walked away, choosing my sanity over impulsive emotions.

You bid me goodbye
and I bid it too
two strangers
who just looked familiar
maybe felt a connection too?

So many thoughts came crashing into my mind, but that was the right thing to do then. I had to take my MBA entrance exam on top of my full-time work. I had to prove myself and make my mom proud. There was no time to waste.

Let us see what life has in hold for me—by taking it one day at a time. I am off to sleep now. Talk to you tomorrow.

Love,
Siddhartha.

22nd Feb, 2021

Dear diary,

Today, the universe conspired to rekindle a spark in my life. I was drawn back to the rooftop terrace, a place still etched in my memory due to the mysterious encounter. And as if by magic, she reappeared, her presence igniting a fire within me.

She was a vision in a flowy yellow dress, her hair cascading down her shoulders like waves, her face aglow with an ethereal light. This time, she was not a fleeting glimpse but a tangible presence—extending a hand forward and requesting to join me. My heart hammered against my ribs, a sensation I had never known before, as this beautiful, enigmatic woman sought my company.

She introduced herself as Alia. Alia, the Jordanian beauty, called the same hotel home as me. Yet, unlike me, she saw it as a temporary haven, a stepping stone in her adventurous journey of life. We spoke for hours, her voice was like a melodic rhythm that held me spellbound. I learned of her aspirations to become an artist, her mind buzzing with a million creative ideas.

As the night deepened, we dived into each other's souls, sharing our dreams and desires. I confessed my yearning to become a poet, reciting verses with a fiery passion. Her response was unique—she translated my words into Arabic, her voice weaving a new tapestry of meaning with each syllable.

Though our conversations flowed effortlessly, a stark contrast emerged as we peeled the layers of our lives. Her desire for simplicity, her contentment with "just enough", clashed with my ambition and my hunger for more in life. She yearned for a quiet haven in the suburbs while I dreamt of towering townhouses and the spotlight.

Despite our differences, I felt drawn to her genuine nature and her ability to find joy in the unimportant things. She was an oasis of calm amidst the chaos of my ambitions, reminding me that happiness does not reside in material possessions.

As the moon painted the rooftop silver, casting long shadows around us, I wished time stood still. We were two souls connected by an invisible thread, sharing secrets under the silent canopy of stars. Her yellow dress, transformed by the moonlight, symbolised purity and hope, mirroring the luminescence in her eyes.

Our encounter left an indelible mark on my soul. It was a chance to see the world through different eyes, a reminder that true fulfilment lies not in chasing fleeting desires but in embracing the simple joys of life.

Once I was done with my poems, she played me her favourite song on YouTube, 'Someone like you':

'I heard that you've settled down
That you found a girl and you're married now
I heard that your dreams came true
Guess she gave you things, I didn't give to you
Old friend, why are you so shy?
Ain't like you to hold back or hide from the light

I hate to turn up out of the blue, uninvited
But I could not stay away, I could not fight it

I had hoped you would see my face
And that you'd be reminded that for me, it isn't over
Never mind, I will find someone like you
I wish nothing but the best for you, too
Do not forget me, "I beg"
I remember you said
"Sometimes it lasts in love, but sometimes it hurts instead"
"Sometimes it lasts in love, but sometimes it hurts instead.""

She played one song, and I played another, and this saga continued until 2 a.m. The stars were still bright and shining, but we were tired and decided to call it a night.

As we parted ways, she smiled at me, and my heart soared. I think this might be the beginning of something unique and magical. I do not want to get ahead of myself, but I cannot deny the spark between us.

Now, I cannot help but wonder if this was the red thread of destiny at work. Only time will tell where this newfound connection will lead us. But for now, I will cherish the memory of our rooftop rendezvous.

She smiled, and I wished for that smile to fall upon me forever.

Love,
Siddhartha.

27th Feb, 2021

Dear diary,

I have been meeting Alia daily on the terrace. We meet at 7 p.m. She gets her Turkish coffee, and I get my energy drink. Then we share about the day and tell each other all the exciting stuff. Once that is over, we dive deeper into conversations. We talk about art, poetry, music, and whatnot.

As we started diving deeper, I explained to her how this career was crucial for me to make money. I did not come from a wealthy background and needed the money to give my mother a good life. However, poetry was a passion that I could pursue with a full-time job.

She has insisted that I open an Instagram page to post my poems. It would help people connect with me and feel that no one is truly alone in this life.

Amid the artificiality, she is a breath of fresh air. There's an unexplainable connection between us, as if we were two lost pieces of a puzzle finally finding each other.

I had never imagined that I would yearn for someone's presence this way. I have grown accustomed to solitude, and finding comfort in the absence of betrayal and heartbreak in life. But with her, everything feels different. Our talks are enthralling and captivating, and I find myself hanging onto her every word.

It is as if the universe has conspired to bring us together at this very moment.

I do not seek a fling or a relationship; I am not willing to open myself up to a potential hurt again. But she makes me question my resolve. Should I risk it all for this newfound connection? Or should I maintain my distance to protect my heart?

Tonight, as we bid goodbyes, I could sense that she wanted to talk more and continue the beautiful conversation. Yet, I held back, knowing that allowing this bond to grow could lead to complications that I was unprepared to handle.

So, with a heavy heart, I bid her goodnight and retreated to my room. It was a difficult decision. I could not ask for her phone number; I cannot afford to complicate my life with unnecessary attachments.

But as I lay here in the stillness of the night, I cannot help but wonder if I am making a mistake. Should I have taken the risk and seized the chance to explore what we have? Or am I simply protecting myself from the potential pain?

I wish I had all the answers. For now, I must tread carefully, protecting my heart while trying to understand the enigma that is this girl. Only time will reveal the path we are meant to take.

Love,
Siddhartha.

Amidst all the chaos that
was happening in my life,
you were the only solace
that was keeping me alive.

Maybe you are right,
and maybe I am not wrong,
our souls collided at a time,
where they did not belong.

01st March, 2021

There is a doubt
bustling inside my heart
that this connection
is somewhere from the past.

Dear diary,

Life has a funny way of surprising us. Just when I thought my heart could not bear any more pain after my breakup, a new friendship blossomed in the most unexpected place. I met her on the rooftop of a hotel in Dubai, the city that held me through the heartache of my past love.

And yet, she brought forth a new light into my life.

We started as mere strangers, but there was an instant connection, something unspoken that drew us together. Her laughter was like a soothing melody that eased the ache in my heart. Her eyes held a depth I could not resist diving into. And in them, I saw a glimmer of understanding, as if she too, had experienced the pain of lost love. She once told me to remember that there is a thread that connects some souls. No matter if they meet or not, they are always one.

Yesterday, we visited Dubai. As we roamed around the city's old streets, our conversations flowed effortlessly. I found myself sharing pieces of my heart with her, something I had not done with anyone since my breakup. It was as if the walls I had built around myself were crumbling, and I felt vulnerable yet safe in her presence. As I looked into her eyes, a million rainbows shined in a universe full of stars, and all of them intertwined.

But life has its own plans, and I am learning to embrace the beauty of this connection without expectations. I see a glimmer of hope in her, reminding me that love comes in many forms and healing can be found in the most unexpected places.

Dubai, a city of dreams and possibilities, has given me a new beginning that I will cherish, even if it does not lead to a romantic love story. For now, I will continue roaming in Dubai's streets, finding solace in her company, and relishing the gift of a friendship that has filled my heart with joy.

I do not want to fall into an abyss this time,
hopelessly waiting and building dreams
whose weight I might have to carry
over endless years
with broken heart and never-ending tears.

Love,
Siddhartha.

If I could ever go back in the past,
I would make sure to ignore you
the first time our eyes met
because
it is killing me: the anxious
and painful wait.

7th March, 2021

Dear diary,

Days have passed without a glimpse of her, and restlessness has consumed me. I tried convincing myself that she meant nothing, but a passing acquaintance. Intense emotional baggage is the last thing I needed, and I do not want to get entangled in unexpected connections.

But Fate had its own plans, and thoughts of her keep invading my mind. I feel powerless against this unbidden attraction, and it has left me feeling helpless. I can't pinpoint the reason for this uneasiness, which only adds to the turmoil.

Why did our paths cross? I wonder. The more I try to push her away, the more she seems to linger in my thoughts. It is a strange dance of emotions that I never asked for, and I cannot escape it.

I was trying to battle my anxiety and the fear of not seeing her ever again is pushing me into a bottomless abyss. We did have a strong connection. Fate wanted to tease me. I had no option but to see what was written in my destiny.

To distract myself from the anxiety, I bury my nose in articles on my phone. But after five minutes, she calls my name from across the pool. Surprisingly, I feel a surge of joy. Relief washes over me as I lay eyes on her once again. Happiness fills my heart as she utters my name. And so, we continue our conversation, talking continuously for six hours.

This is happening to me for the second time in my life. I remember how I had fallen head over heels with Siya, and now with her. I feel scared and tell myself daily not to talk to her, because it could lead to a disaster. But as they say, the heart wants what it wants.

But do not think I did not study today. I returned to my room, and before writing here, I studied for hours. I am off to sleep now, diary. I am exhausted.

Love,
Siddhartha.

You were drug to my soul and that
is why I was craving for you just
one more time.

20th March, 2021

You were like a moon in my universe
as
I could only know you from a distance.

Dear diary,

Things are moving fast now, as if I am in some movie. We have become friends in such a short span. Finally, we have exchanged numbers. She is my first text in the morning and the last good night. Throughout the day, we text and keep each other updated about on our whereabouts.

I do not know how she feels about me, but I like her. Whenever we are about to meet, I feel like a teenager. I feel the butterflies swirling in my stomach until my eyes find her in the crowd.

Sometimes, we just bask in the silence and do our work. I have told her about my dreams and the MBA plan; and she has told me to not waste time in talking to her and to focus on my studies. So now I take my books and study next to her on the rooftop while she watches videos on her phone. We like seeing each other, and we feel content.

Yesterday, a strange thing happened. She called me to the rooftop around 6:30 p.m. Generally, we meet at 7 p.m. She sounded a bit tense, so without wasting time, I went upstairs. I saw her from a distance; she looked sad, and I could also notice that she was crying. The moment she saw me, she came running into my arms.

Shocked, I did not know how to respond. I used to think that I was alive, but the moment she hugged me, I felt like I had not been alive in years, and she brought oxygen into my lungs. After a few minutes, I enquired what happened.

Tears continuously trickled down her skin, and I took the courage to wipe them off. Her blue eyes wanted to say something, but her lips could not. I did not ask anything. After some time, she asked me if we could drive around, as she needed some fresh air. In the car, I played a song that she liked in a low volume.

My car had not smelled so nice in years. It was her perfume. I could smell her. I looked at her and noticed that her tears had not stopped. After some time, I parked my car near the hotel parking to comfort her. There was a silence that was not peaceful. I did not know how to feel at that moment. I knew something was wrong, but I did not know how to ask or console Alia if she did share something.

In that silence, I was trying to think what could be wrong. A million things were running in my mind, but thankfully, Alia broke the silence.

Alia: She called.

Me: Who called?

Alia: You do not know her. She is my aunt. She called me. She got my number from my mother.

Me: Okay. So, what is the problem?

Alia: She is in Dubai and wants to meet me.

Me: Okay…

Alia: (Crying profusely) I cannot meet her.

Me: Why? What happened?

Alia: She… she…

Me: What? She does what?

Alia: Would you believe if I tell you the truth?

Me: Of course, why not.

Alia: Because my parents did not. They thought I was lying.

Me: Tell me. I believe you. I do not know why your parents did not believe. I believe you.

Alia: She is not a nice woman. She…

Me: Did she do something bad to you?

By this time, Alia was shaking. She took my hand and told me to calm her down. She told me to feel her heart as she was afraid of how it was beating. I did not know what to say. I felt so hopeless. I urged Alia to tell me the truth.

Alia: When I was a kid, this aunty came to our house in Jordan. She is my mother's cousin's sister. As we had two rooms in the house, she shared mine during the night. When everyone was asleep, she touched me inappropriately and took a promise from me to not tell anyone.

One day, I could not take it anymore, and I told my mother. But she did not believe me. She told me her sister could never do this, and I was making stuff up to get attention. I cried for hours. But my mother discussed this with my aunt, and she never came to our house after that day. It's been 20 years, and now she has called me.

I did not utter a word. I was shocked to the core and could only imagine how Alia would have felt.

Me: Whatever I say would not be enough to seal your pain, but do not pick up her call ever again. I don't know why your mother did not believe you. But I trust you, and I believe everything that you have told me. I do not know if we will be in touch forever, but remember, I will always protect you. You can share anything with me, Alia. I promise to not judge you.

There was a silence after this. We only spoke for a short time. She kept weeping, and I did not think it was appropriate to advise her anything. She needed someone to share this dark secret, and I was glad that she chose me. After some time, she told me that she will block her aunt. She mentioned that she had never shared this incident with anyone but me, and I could not help feeling glad. This whole episode made me feel so connected to her. She trusted me, and this was enough for me at the moment.

Love,
Siddhartha.

There were words
even in our silence,
and I know
we were about to fall in love.

21st March, 2021

Dear diary,

Yesterday, Alia and I started talking about random stuff, and out of nowhere, she asked me about my past. I felt a sudden pain in my chest, as all the memories of Siya came crashing down on me.

Alia: So, have you ever loved someone?

Me: I loved her so much that it would be a shame to even talk about it.

Alia: Wow. So, what was your story? Tell me, I want to know.

Me: It is a sad story. It will spoil your mood, leave it.

Alia: I really want to know. I want to experience what love meant for you and why you did not get it in return.

Me: Umm, okay. But it is a sad, unfinished love story.

Alia: No! Tell me in detail. What happened? How did you meet her?

Me: Where do I start…

> Her smokey eyes
> colourful skies
> she smirked a little, gave me butterflies

I laid my eyes
on her pretty face
her innocence
enchanted me into a happy space.

Alia: Was she so beautiful?

Me: Saying that she was just beautiful will not do justice to her beauty.

Alia: So, you just loved her because she was pretty?

Me: She gave me the vibe
and I knew it was real,
in this fake modern world
she looked clear and
almost surreal.

Alia: But how did you know that you were in love?

Me: Her heartbeat
synchronised with mine,
and I knew I was in love
when I saw her for the first time.

Alia: But why did you love her?

Me: It was not about the intimacy,
kisses, or fantasy,
she told me her secrets
which she had not told anyone before
and I do not know what people think
but for me, it was more than love.

Alia: Then what happened? I get it, you were deeply in love with her. But what about her? Did she love you back?

Me: She loved me too and we got engaged soon after. We spent those three years very happily, until...

Alia: Until what?

Me: I am cursed. Happiness does not stay with me for long.
For once in my lifetime,
I thought I had met someone real
and then, her mask fell off.
Alia: Why? What did she do?

Me: She blackened my days
darkened my nights
and when I said "I loved you,"
she coldly looked into my eyes
making me sound so stupid
as if our love was nothing but a game.
but because she cheated,
she is the one to be blamed.

Alia: Oh, I am so sorry. Why did she cheat?

Me: She thought that the other guy could give her a more promising future than I could ever give. He was from a top engineering college, and I was just an average person studying in a local college.

Alia: That is incredibly sad. What happened next?

Me: I begged and begged, but it was all in vain.
I said to her, "But I love you.
Is it not enough?"
"Shy love is never enough," she said and left.
And at that moment I knew our love was over. It was a mirage and nothing else.

Alia: This is heart wrenching. You must have been depressed. What did you do?

Me: She pushed me into the darkness. I stayed there for months, always thinking about how…

Her name still sparked my eyes
And it gave me butterflies
she said love happens just once,
so how come she fell in love twice.

I started smoking, drinking, and did not think about anything other than her. I used to cry and wait for her to call me once and apologise. She did call me after many months. She wanted to come back and thought leaving me was a mistake, as the other person did not love her as much as I did. Apparently, he cheated on her.

Alia: Why did you not move on with someone else?

Me: My heart was still stuck on her,
my mind told me to move on,
move on with someone new,
my only worry was,
what if the girl I end up moving on with
turned out to be just like her.

I tried to move on
but could not. Then one day
I cried and cried and cried and just like that,
my tears stopped,
and she was no longer the someone I wanted to hold.

Alia: This is so sad. I am sorry, but I can't help wanting to know more.

Me: The journey from "I am glad to meet you"
to "I wonder why I met you"
was unbearably painful
to be told in simple words,
Hence, I will leave it up to you to think
Why our love story did not work?

Alia: Do you still believe in soulmates?

Me: In the luscious green fields
where the cloudy skies
meet the aqua seas, I will find my soulmate there.

Love,
Siddhartha.

22nd March, 2021

We were two hearts and one soul
she broke my dreams
and I do not know where to go.

Dear diary,
As I shared my love story with Alia, a wave of sadness washed over me. The memories of my past life flooded back, and I felt like I had no control over them. It took me two long years to overcome that heartbreak, and I believed that I had moved on. I thought her memories would not haunt me anymore, but I was wrong.

Suddenly, I found myself missing Siya all over again. I wish she had not betrayed me; I wish we were still together, and things had turned out differently. The pain of the past still lingers on, and I cannot help but wonder what could have been.

I yearn to hold her close, to feel the warmth of her embrace, but I know it can never be true. Our paths have diverged, and I must accept that we are no longer meant to be.

But even amidst the sadness, I remind myself that I have survived heartbreak once before, and I can do so again. Time will heal these wounds, and I will find the strength to move forward, even if her memories continue to stay in the corners of my heart.

I have always found healing in time. I grew up with a broken heart. I never felt close to my father until he went to the hospital when I was eight. He changed after that. Maybe he had realised he did not have much time left. He came back from the hospital and started to spend time with me. He still mistreated my mother, which hurt me a lot, but he was different to me. Two years went by, and I turned ten.

I remember it was the day of my last exam, and I came home and watched TV. My mother was still at school, and my father had gone to meet a client in another town. My grandmother gave me lunch, and I fell asleep.

After 10 minutes, the phone rang, and I ran to answer it. The person on the other side asked for an adult. My mother arrived just then and took the call. She woke up my grandmother and told her some upsetting news. My father had been taken to a hospital in Noida. He said that it was nothing serious but wanted us to come as soon as possible. I still remember the ride to the hospital. I sat next to my mother. It was a freezing evening, and the sun was almost down. My mother was crying nonstop as if she had had a hunch. I felt unfortunate. We got to the hospital, and a nurse led us to the room. I expected to see my dad hooked up to machines and wires, but I was wrong. He lay there with his eyes shut. I thought he was asleep. My mother screamed, and I was confused. After a while, a doctor came in and said that my father had suffered a massive heart attack, and he could not be saved.

That was the first time I saw a dead body. I was terrified but also relieved. I was relieved from the pain of watching my parents fight all the time, relieved from being yelled at, relieved from being afraid of him, and relieved from some hidden pain. I knew then that my life had changed, and I wanted to do everything to make my mother happy and proud. I tried everything to make her smile and forget the pain that he had caused her. A voice in my head kept talking to me, and I could not stop it. That voice stayed with me until I became depressed when I was sixteen.

Lately, I have been hearing that voice again. The voice tells me to prove myself. The voice tells me to make my mother happy and proud. The voice that tells me to get rid of my flaws.

I want to give my mother a good life. She gave me everything. I want to see pride in her eyes reflecting that she raised me well. I will not let anything distract me. Not even Siya's memories.

Love,
Siddhartha.

24th March, 2021

Someone reminded me of her!
and that one thought
ruined my world.

Dear diary,

After I shared my love story with Alia, she looked at me with concern and asked what had happened to me. I was at a loss for words, unable to express the baggage of thoughts that had resurfaced. Yet, somehow, she seemed to understand, and she gently apologised for bringing up those memories.

To lighten the mood, she suggested we go to a *sheesha* place. I hesitated initially, unsure if I was ready for distractions, but she insisted and I gave in. We found ourselves in a cozy sheesha lounge, ordering Turkish food, Turkish coffee, and sheesha. As we sat there, the aroma of the *hookah* and the sound of laughter created a soothing ambiance.

Alia tried to make me smile, cracking silly jokes and sharing amusing anecdotes. Despite my sadness, I could not help but laugh at her infectious innocence. I felt like she was trying to mend the broken pieces of my heart, and for a brief moment, I forgot the pain I had.

The hours flew by and we lost track of time, still talking in the car even after we had returned to our hotel. The conversation flowed effortlessly, and I opened up to her more than I had ever expected. Our connection felt natural, as if we had known each other for years.

May the hands of time stand still,
may the world come to a
pause,
until
then I will pour my heart.

As we bid each other goodnight, I realised that Alia had unknowingly brought a glimmer of light back into my life. Despite the sadness, I felt a sense of gratitude for her presence, reminding me that laughter and connection can heal even the deepest wounds.

She bid me goodbye,
and I bid her bye too
was I falling for her?
when my heart was shouting not to.

Love,
Siddhartha.

25th March, 2021

I craved for intimacy, and
she touched my soul
and I knew she is all I ever need.

Dear diary,

Yesterday, we decided to take a stroll at the Dubai Creek. As we headed over to the Creek side, we found ourselves stuck amidst a crowd for a light show. Concerned, I instinctively moved closer to her. But in that fleeting moment, something happened that I never saw coming.

As I leaned in to hold her hand, I found myself mere inches away from her face, and a surge of passion washed over me. Time seemed to stand still as our breaths mingled, and I felt a connection like never before in that proximity. It was as if every heartbeat echoed with a longing to be near her, to feel her presence so close to mine.

My hands trembled, not from fear but from the moment's intensity. For years, I had kept a distance from forming such close connections, guarding my heart from potential hurt. But in that fleeting moment, all my walls came crashing down, and I could not deny the sensations that stirred within me.

As I drew near,
so close to you
unfelt passion,
something new
your breath brushed
gently on my face
a sensation I will never erase
what was stirring deep inside me?

A wind of feelings,
I could not hide in your presence,
I had a chance
my heart filled with dance of emotions,
maybe for a romance?

It was a sudden realisation, knowing that this unexpected closeness had awakened something inside me that I thought was long dormant of. As we continued our evening, I tried my best to maintain composure, but my heart still fluttered with the memory of that brief, unguarded moment.

I am left wondering that I can no longer resist her magnetic pull on me. No matter how hard I try to suppress these feelings, they persist, growing stronger by each passing day. As I sit here, lost in the depth of my thoughts, I cannot help but wonder what this encounter means and where will it lead us in this journey of life.

Love,
Siddhartha.

A feeling so new,
little ticklish,
little strange,
a romance in the making
or maybe a wild mistake?

26th May, 2021

I wonder if I am ever in
your mind like you are
In mine literally all
the time.

Dear diary,

The last four months with Alia have been a rollercoaster ride, creating a sense of familiarity that spans years. Every time I am with her, time seems to slip away, and I find myself yearning for more. Yesterday was no different; I could not wait to see her again.

As I stood there, waiting for her to emerge from her office, my heart raced with anticipation.

It was a feeling I had not experienced in years, reminiscent of the time when I used to eagerly wait for Siya in college. The restlessness inside me was so intense that I could hardly contain. It felt like an eternity until Alia finally appeared, and as soon as our eyes met, a rush of emotions surged through me. It was as if every cell in my body recognised her. She was holding a cup in her hand when she entered my car. On asking, I learned that she went to a new boutique coffee shop, and it was serving hot chocolate with whipped cream, which was my favourite.

I had told Alia a couple of days back about the drink, and not only did she remember, but she even bought it for me. I felt so happy, and the first sip itself took me to winter.

As we embarked on our evening plans to the open night market, I cherished every moment with her. Our laughter filled the air, and I could not help being drawn to her magnetic presence. I felt a sense of comfort and familiarity with her, as if we had shared a lifetime of memories.

While walking, Alia opened her bag and gave me a pen drive.

Me: What is inside this pen drive?
Alia: It may sound cheesy, but I made a playlist for you. It has all my favourite songs that I think you might like as well.

No one had ever done anything like this for me. And suddenly, this incident took me years back to when I made a movie of sorts for Siya wherein, I had put all our pictures and edited songs over them. I wanted to show her how special she was, and I still remember the smile on Siya's face when she had seen that movie for the first time.

Suddenly, I saw Alia snapping her fingers at me to bring me back to reality. I came to my senses, and I saw the warmth in her eyes. I gazed at her for a reasonable amount of time because I did not even feel like anyone else was in that market, besides me and Alia.

I do not have words to express what I felt at that moment, but I knew that Alia had found a way into the deepest chambers of my soul. It was an intensity of feelings I had not experienced in a long time, leaving me vulnerable yet exhilarated.

These feelings are both thrilling and terrifying as I navigate this uncharted territory with Alia. But I cannot deny her pull on me, and I am excited to see where this intense journey will lead us.

Love,
Siddhartha.

My eyes did roam
to search for her
and then suddenly
I saw her in
the crowd
behind so many smiles
and my soul whispered,
here comes your forever.

27th May, 2021

You stole my breath away
and asked me
to stay alive.
how?

Dear diary,

Curiosity led us to a quaint little shop where Alia's friend, a palmist held the key to uncovering the secrets in our palms. I watched as Alia's eyes sparkled with excitement. She was piqued to know what the lines of her hand held.

As the palmist examined Alia's palm, I stood by her side, curious yet sceptical about the revelations to come. The friend's eyes flicked up, her gaze settling on me. With an all-knowing smile, she inquired about Alia's "boyfriend".

The words struck me like a bolt of lightning, unexpected and electrifying. I glanced at Alia, my surprise mirroring hers. I did not know Alia's romantic history, and the revelation left me speechless. My mind raced, trying to reconcile the picture before me with the woman I had come to know.

Alia paused, her eyes meeting mine for a fleeting moment. Then, in a measured tone, she admitted that their relationship had been on and off, marked by complexities and challenges. She stated that she would only consider rekindling their connection if he convinced his parents to accept their union.

The palmist's words flowed like a river of prophecy, weaving a surreal tale. She spoke of potential breakups, only to face their obstacles. Each word seemed like a twist in the fabric of fate, and I could not help but feel a shiver down my spine.

Amidst the predictions, Alia's resolve remained unshaken. With a determined glint in her eyes, she insisted that she wanted to marry her boyfriend, regardless of the challenges ahead. It was as if the palmist's words were mere echoes against the fortress of her determination.

As we left the shop, I felt something like an undefined swirling within me. The unexpected revelations, a glimpse into Alia's past, and unwavering conviction about her future, all weaved a complex tapestry. Alia's heart was steadfast and unyielding in the face of the palmist's predictions.

During it all, I found myself grappling with questions about the future and the path ahead for both of us. As we walked away from the palmist's realm, the echoes of her words lingered in the air. It was a reminder that destiny's tapestry was woven with threads of uncertainty, surprise, and a dash of unwavering love.

Love,
Siddhartha.

01st June, 2021

You were real
and so was I
then why our story
before even taking off
died.

Dear diary,

It has been a while since I poured my heart out, and right now, I am drowning in a sea of emotions that are hard to express. The pain I am feeling is overwhelming, and I do not know where to start.

I had believed that the connection between Alia and me was something special, something mutual. But life's complexities have cruelly shattered that illusion.

Today, during our conversation after the visit to the palm reader, Alia confessed that she is already involved with someone else. Someone that she has been in an on-and-off relationship with, for a staggering three years. Hearing those words felt like a sharp dagger being thrust into my chest, leaving me gasping for breath. My mind was racing, replaying every moment we spent together, trying to decipher if there were any signs that I had missed. I thought she felt the same way about me, but I was mistaken.

Maybe her eyes never lied.
My stupid heart made up a love
that never existed in the first place.

Her eyes, a swirling ocean of sadness, spoke volumes of a love lost. Tears flowed freely, a silent river for the man she cherished more than anything else. Hamza, his name whispered like a secret prayer, was the anchor of her heart, a love story etched in the halls of their college.

Distance, a cruel enemy, loomed over their bond. Fearful of its icy grip on their love, Hamza opposed Alia's dream of working in Dubai. Yet, her passion burned bright, defying the miles that separated them. So safe was Hamza in her heart that his name remained unspoken, a sacred treasure guarded within.

Marriage, a distant promise in Alia's eyes, clashed with Hamza's yearning for immediate commitment. His persistent pleas for her to return to Jordan fuelled their fiery arguments. Amid their tumultuous journey, fleeting thoughts of parting ways arose, only to be dispelled by fleeting moments of reconciliation.

But today, the echo of a palmist's chilling prophecy reverberated through Alia's soul. The ominous threat of a potential breakup casted a dark shadow upon her heart, filling it with fear and uncertainty. Lost in the labyrinth of her thoughts, she poured out her story, oblivious to the storm brewing within me.

Consumed by the flames of unrequited love, I fought back the tears that threatened to spill. Her trust and desire for a solid foundation before unveiling her vulnerability resonated with me. Yet, the stark reality of her love for another person, pierced me like a thousand shards of glass.

The weight of my shattered heart felt unbearable. The path ahead stretched before me, a daunting, uncertain landscape. Unrequited love, a bitter pill to swallow, left a taste of despair upon my tongue. But amidst the darkness, just a flicker of hope remained.

Time, the relentless healer would mend the wounds, I believed. Perhaps, somewhere beyond the horizon, a love destined for me awaited. But for now, I embraced the pain, allowing it to wash over me in cleansing waves.

As I met her gaze, devoid of understanding, I yearned for her to feel the agony that was tearing me apart. Her questions, a gentle prod into my silent suffering, were met with a fabricated response, a shield against further vulnerability.

The silence that followed was deafening, like a chasm between our hearts. And as I turned away, I carried the weight of my unrequited love—a burden I knew I had to bear, until time, the ultimate healer intervened.

Love,
Siddhartha.

Can you look away?
There is something in my eyes
I know you can see my tears but let us just pretend
I am doing all right.

10th June, 2021

Dear diary,

It has been ten long days since I last saw Alia. She has been messaging me relentlessly, wanting to meet, but I cannot face her. I am scared that if we meet, my true feelings will pour out, and she will realise how deeply I love her. I do not know what to do; I feel lost and alone, with no one to confide in about the heartache I am going through.

After my painful breakup with Siya, I thought I had finally found a chance at love with Alia. But then, she revealed that she was in love with someone else. It felt like my heart had been ripped apart all over again, and I could not bear to see her, knowing that I would have to hide my true feelings.

I wish she had told me the truth earlier, and so I would not have created stories and false hopes in my mind. Maybe then, I would not be drowning in this heart-wrenching pain, feeling like I have lost the chance at happiness once more. As I walk alone through the streets of Dubai, memories of our time together flood my mind, and I cannot help but wonder if I will ever find someone who understands and loves me, the way I love her.

I am running out of reasons to avoid her, so I had to call her today. She was so excited to tell me about all the latest news in her life. We talked for about ten hours yesterday, and she had to skip office because of that.

She changed like seasons
almost leaving my life without a reason,
and here I am chained behind the walls
my heart crawling away from my soul,
can someone please open the locked door?

Love,
Siddhartha.

What if you looked into my eyes
and asked me to shout your
name, what if you opened my
heart and saw your face
on every page.

11th June, 2021

Dear diary,

I was coming from my office and saw Alia at the reception. She had come to replace the key card as it was not working due to technical challenges.

I saw her from a distance and felt my world crumble upon hearing her magical voice. I did not want to see her afraid of what was to come, but there she was, standing with a glow that I had never seen on her face before. Maybe she was in love, and I wouldn't say now that I like the fateful day when we met for the first time.

Today, Alia asked me to accompany her to the rooftop, and I could not find it in me to refuse. The moment we reached there, an awkward silence settled between us, and my heart felt heavy with the unspoken words. I wanted to tell her everything, share the pain I had been feeling, but words eluded past me. Instead,

I made up an excuse about needing to study and rushed back to my room, leaving her behind.

My hands shivered,
echoing my heart's ache,
tears welled up, emotions at stake
how can I convey my love so deep,
a secret I would always keep.

Since then, I have been burying myself in my studies, using them as a shield to distract myself from the pain. My GMAT exam is just around the corner, and I know I cannot afford to let my feelings get the better of me. There is so much at stake, and my dreams await me. I have to focus on building my future and achieving my goals, and that means putting aside the thoughts of Alia.

It is not easy, I know. Whenever I try to study, memories of her keep creeping into my mind, making it hard to concentrate. But I cannot let this heartbreak define me. I have a life to build, and it is up to me to make it something extraordinary.

The journey ahead may be challenging, but I believe in myself. I know I can overcome this pain and longing and turn it into something positive. I will not let the love loss deter me from reaching my full potential.

So, I take a deep breath, steel my resolve, and return to my studies. I will focus on my future and work hard to achieve my dreams. And who knows, someday, I will find someone who truly appreciates me for who I am and what I have to offer.

For now, though, I will take it one step at a time. I will stay strong and keep moving forward, knowing that the best is yet to come. My heart may be broken, but I will not let it break my spirit. I have a life to build and am ready to embrace it with open arms.

Back to studies again.

Love,
Siddhartha.

I do not know
If a parallel world exists
and we still have a chance
to reconnect and build
what we could not
on this parallel side

12th June, 2021

Dear diary,

Today, as I stood on the rooftop, the wind ruffling my hair and the city lights twinkling below, Alia asked me a question that pierced through the layers of my carefully constructed persona. She had asked, "Why are you so obsessed with proving yourself and going to the USA?"

My heart pounded in my chest as I looked into her curious eyes, her words echoing the doubts that had gnawed at me for years. How could I articulate the tumultuous journey that had led me to this moment, the struggles that had shaped my determination, the dreams that fuelled my relentless ambition?

I was an ordinary, unremarkable, and unmemorable boy until ten. That is when fate, in a cruel twist, snatched away my father, leaving a void that remained throughout my young life. Overnight, I was transformed into a miniature adult, carrying the weight of my mother's hopes and dreams on my slender shoulders.

Academic excellence became my obsession and my armour against the world's harsh realities. I excelled in school. My mind was a whirlwind of formulas and equations, and my heart was constantly yearning for the validation that I was worthy, and that I mattered.

The pressure mounted as I entered standard XI when I had to start preparing for the gateway to India's elite Engineering institutions, the IITs. Those bastions of intellectual prowess loomed before me, their daunting entrance exams casting a shadow over my every waking moment.

But the burden proved too heavy to bear. The weight of expectations, the fear of failure, and the relentless self-imposed pressure crushed my spirit, leaving me paralysed with anxiety and self-doubt. I remember the tears and the silent sobs that accompanied me as I wrestled with every chapter, every equation, and every concept that seemed to elude my grasp.

Defeated, I accepted my fate, settling for a lesser institution where my mediocrity would blend seamlessly with the crowd. I trudged through my Engineering degree, a shadow of the student I once aspired to be.

Then came Siya, a beacon of light in my otherwise monotonous existence. But even love, with its intoxicating promises and fleeting joys, could not erase the gnawing emptiness within me. When our relationship crumbled, I was left adrift, a rudderless ship in a tumultuous sea.

It was in the depths of that despair that I found the courage to confront my inner demons. I confided in Aditya, my confidant and my rock, and he guided me towards healing.

A diagnosis of Obsessive Compulsive Disorder (OCD) opened my eyes to the invisible enemy that had been sabotaging my life. The overwhelming anxiety, the debilitating fear of failure, the relentless pursuit of perfection—these were not signs of weakness but symptoms of a condition that I could manage, if not control.

With medication and therapy, I embarked on a journey of self-discovery, learning to tame the unruly thoughts that had held me captive for so long. The transformation was gradual, but it was real. The fog that had clouded my mind began to lift, revealing a glimmer of hope and determination.

The GMAT, the gateway to my American dream, became my next Everest. Armed with newfound clarity and unwavering resolve, I plunged into the world of verbal and quantitative reasoning, determined to conquer this new challenge.

My first attempt yielded a decent score, but it fell short of the lofty standards of the institutions I aspired to attend. Undeterred, I sought refuge in Dubai, a city of dreams and possibilities. Here, amidst the towering skyscrapers and bustling streets, I found a new home where I could reinvent myself, free from the shackles of past failures.

Aditya, my ever-present anchor, guided me through the labyrinthine world of GMAT preparation. We dissected each question, analysed each strategy, and pushed each other to our limits. I also met many remarkable individuals who shared my passion, drive, and insatiable hunger for knowledge.

The second attempt yielded a modest improvement, but more was needed. Yet, I remained undeterred, my resolve strengthened by each setback. In mock exams, I soared to new heights, my scores inching closer to 750, the benchmark that I had set for myself.

The road ahead is long and arduous, but I am no longer the timid boy who trembled under the weight of expectations. I am a seasoned warrior with resilience, determination, and a newfound understanding of my strengths and my limitations.

I will conquer this GMAT. I will silence the voices of doubt that have haunted me for so long. I will prove to myself, my mother, and the world that I can achieve the extraordinary.

Wish me luck, diary, for I am on the brink of something extraordinary.

Love,
Siddhartha.

25th June, 2021

Dear diary,

Tomorrow is the big day. My exam is finally here, and the weight of this moment bears down on me. It has been a whole month since I last saw Alia, but I know I made the right decision to focus on my studies. She understood and promised to pray for me, and that gesture meant the world.

I have not asked her about her relationship yet. Honestly, I do not have the heart to do so. My mind is consumed with thoughts of the exam, and I cannot afford any distractions right now. I have also taken leave from my job to dedicate every waking moment to studying, putting in ten to fifteen hours each day to ensure that I am fully prepared. I can get my target score in the mock exams, but the actual exam is a different ball game all together.

The anxiety is palpable, and it feels like time is slipping through my fingers. I have worked very hard for this exam, pouring months of effort into my preparation. I want to achieve my desired score, and pay off all my hard work.

As the day draws nearer, I feel a mix of nerves and excitement. I have a dream to fulfil and this exam is the stepping stone to that future. I want to make my mom proud, and show her that her sacrifices were worth it.

The road ahead will not be easy, and there are moments when the pain of heartbreak threatens to overwhelm me. But I remind myself that being strong is my only option. I cannot afford to waste time on anything that will not lead me closer to my goals.

I am proud of myself for staying focused and determined, even in the face of heartache. It has not been easy, but I know this is the path I must walk. Tomorrow, I will give it my all, leaving nothing behind. I will chase my dreams with every ounce of strength I have.

Wish me luck, dear diary. Tommorow, I hope that my efforts will be enough to open doors to the best B-Schools in the USA. I hope I will beat the GMAT, even when all the odds are against me.

Love,
Siddhartha.

I was at the edge of getting lost
and she was the way
I was searching for
in my life, but she was
home for someone else
hence, I woke up.

26th June, 2021

Dear diary,

The morning of the exam is nerve-wracking. My heart was pounding so loudly that I could hardly hear my thoughts. I barely slept last night, and by 6 a.m., I was already wide awake. To ease my anxiety, I decided to meditate. It helped to calm my mind a little, but the jittery feeling persisted. I managed to squeeze in a quick hour of sleep after meditation, which refreshed my mind. Today is the third time when I will appear for my exam.

With my phone switched off, I went to the exam centre. I kept to myself, not engaging in any conversation to maintain my focus. The exam was nothing short of challenging. But I did not let the tough questions deter me. I faced each problem with unwavering confidence and a sense of calmness. Slowly but steadily, I made my way through the exam, refusing to give in to any panic.

A sense of relief washed over me when I finally finished and submitted my paper. But my fate now rested in that score, and my heart was pounding again. As I said a silent prayer, I felt overwhelmed. I checked my score, and to my disbelief, it read 760/800. I could not believe my eyes. I had done it. I began crying. I could not contain them, they were tears of joy and triumph. So, I let them flow.

My heart burst with happiness. I called my mom, and we talked for hours. She understood my struggle to reach this point, and her tears of joy echoed mine. And then, I knew I had to share this moment with Alia. She had been there through my difficult time and had also sent me a heartfelt text wishing me luck.

As I ascended the rooftop, she stood, looking as radiant as ever. I could not contain my excitement, and joy streamed down my cheeks as I shared my score with her. She understood the significance of this moment for me as I had told her that this would be my third attempt. She hugged me tightly, expressing her happiness and pride in my achievement.

As others noticed my tears, someone came over to check if I was okay. Little did they know that these were tears of triumph and overcoming adversity and pain. I had fought hard to get here. Now, I could finally celebrate my victory.

I did it, dear diary, I did it. I beat the OCD and the heartache.

Love,
Siddhartha.

27th June, 2021

Dear diary,

Today, I feel like a bird set free from its cage. The weight of months and years of hard work and stress has lifted, and I can finally breathe.

With my sights set on the future, I have decided to travel to the USA to explore business schools, seeking inspiration for my impactful essays. I still have three months before the deadline, so I allowed myself the luxury of relaxation, something I have not experienced in a long while. But then the reality of Alia came crashing in. I just remembered Hamza, and even though this man has not done anything to me, I hate him. How can he love Alia? I felt Alia and I belonged together. I knew her from some past life, and now here I am, just as a friend of hers.

I saw Alia on a call with Hamza, and they were disagreeing on something. I was boiling with jealousy on seeing Alia talk to someone else than me. She was in her office clothes. She came straight to the terrace after work. She was wearing smart casuals and had straightened her hair that day. With that hair, she seemed like a banker.

After the call, I asked Alia if she wanted to join me for an Open Mic night, and to my delight, she agreed. Little did she know that the poems I had prepared, were crafted with her in mind. I tried to forget that Alia had someone in her life, and for once in months, I wanted to enjoy that evening with her.

It was a surreal experience to pour my feelings through those beautiful lines, and she listened intently, oblivious to their true meaning. The night was pure magic as I recited three heartfelt poems. My heart swelled with joy and nervousness, knowing that each word was a testament to my feelings for Alia.

After the performance, we bid each other goodnight, and as she left, a surge of unexplainable feelings filled me. I could not resist the urge to write one more poem that spoke of our connection and the bond between us.

Let us meet again
maybe at a right time
and we will tell what is in our minds
till then I will hold a place for you in my heart
because I am too afraid for a fresh start.

In that moment, I felt a sense of belonging, a profound connection that words alone could not describe. Alia had become my muse, and through my poetry, I could express the depths of what I felt for her. I did not know if she understood the significance of those verses, but it did not matter. For in that magical night, our souls danced in harmony, and my heart swelled with a newfound hope for the future.

As I lay down to rest, my mind was abuzz with the enchanting moments we shared. The night had been extraordinary, and my heart was eager to embrace whatever lay ahead. With each word

I penned and poured onto the paper, I felt a sense of release, as if I had finally unburdened my heart.

In the quiet solitude of the night, I found solace in my poetry, and in Alia, I found a connection that I knew was meant to be cherished. The journey had just begun, and I was eager to see where it would lead us. And thus I went to sleep, my heart full of the melodies of my poems and the hope of a future intertwined with Alia's presence.

Love,
Siddhartha.

30th June, 2021

Dear diary,

After the poetry night, I only saw Alia a few days ago. It is better to keep some distance as I felt very hurt when I was with her. There were some instances where she brought up Hamza's name, or Hamza called. She told me that she does not share anything about Hamza with anyone, but now, she trusts me and will tell me about her past.

However, I met Alia today after four days, and her eyes were red. It was as if she had been crying for hours. Upon enquiring, I learned that her boyfriend's mother disapproved of their relationship, and he did not want to fight anymore. I had never asked, but this was the main reason they had been in and off a relationship. Today, her mother had put a final nail in the coffin and asked him to choose Alia or her, and he decided to let go of Alia. She was unbearably sad, and I could not see her tears.

I tried my best to offer comfort, saying, "Don't cry. Sometimes, things aren't meant to be."

Alia's voice trembled as she replied, "But I loved him. We were together for three years."

Understanding her pain all too well, I shared, "I know the depth of that hurt. I have stood where you are now. She walked away after three years as though I held no significance."

Her voice quivering, Alia confided, "I can't imagine my life without him."

I reassured her, "You'll find your way, I promise. Look at me—I was once in your shoes and have managed to find my footing again. It is not the end of the world."

It's difficult to witness someone you love shedding tears for another person, right before you. She was my world, but her world was someone else. I wish I had dared to tell her how much I love her and to what extent I could go for her. But I did not, because the time was not right to pour my heart out. Especially when she was already weeping.

What if she could not love me the way I loved her? What if she chose to be alone for her own heart? What if she did not realise what she meant to me still? I will wait till death tears us apart.

I consoled her and tried to make her smile, but all in vain. I know what she was going through and how long it would take her to come out of it, but I decided to be with her on this journey, because she needed me more than I could ever need her.

Love,
Siddhartha.

If I could make a wish
come true,
I would ask my lucky stars
to live an eternity with you.

04th July, 2021

Dear Diary,

Alia needed space after the breakup, and I respected her need for alone time. However, deep down, I could not bear the thought of her being so sad and vulnerable. I knew her well enough to sense that if left on her own, she might spiral into depression. The pain of seeing her like this shattered me into pieces, and all I wanted was to be there for her, to offer comfort and support during her darkest days.

She was lost in the darkness, cold as a stone. She would not utter a word and wanted no one around.

I only wanted to make her smile. I do not know what I mean to her, but I consider her my life.

Love,
Siddhartha.

Why are you pretending
that you are sober
pretending that you are fine
when your clothes smell of dust
and your breath smells of rose wine?

05th July, 2021

Dear diary,

My heart was heavy with sadness as I listened to Alia's teary voice on the phone. Her parents who live far away in Jordan, are calling her back, pressurising her to get married and settle down. It feels like all the problems in the world are converging on us, and I am left feeling helpless and lost.

She sobbed inconsolably, and I wished I could be there to hold her close, to wipe away her tears. I tried my best to offer some comfort, to be the voice of reason in this storm. I suggested that she should go to Jordan and ask her parents for some time. Time to think things through and find a way to express her dreams and desires.

She was as pure as she can be
surreal than my dream
I wish I could hold her and take
away all her pains but then I
remember she can possibly never
be with me.

Maybe her parents will understand and agree to give her some time to make the right decision. It is a small glimmer of hope in the darkness, and I hold onto it tightly, praying that it will lead us to a solution. But the uncertainty and fear weigh heavily on my heart, and I cannot help but feel overwhelmed by the situation. All I want is to see Alia happy, but the road ahead is uncertain, and I fear that the odds are stacked against us.

And hope is all I need for now.

Love,
Siddhartha.

If only she could realise
what she means to me,
we could be a forever.

8th July, 2021

Dear Diary,

As Alia agreed to go to Jordan, my heart sank with emptiness. I was happy that she decided to confront her parents and discuss her priorities, but at the same time, I could not shake the fear of the unknown. What if her parents never let her come back? What if this is the last time, I would ever see her face-to-face?

Restlessness consumed me as I tried to hold back tears. The thought of losing her, even temporarily, felt unbearable. But I knew I had no choice but to let her go, to give her the space she needed to figure out what she genuinely wanted.

I do not know
If I will ever be able to see you again
and my heart is crying in pain
I can neither forget you
nor will I ever do
I will always remember that you
became the sunshine to my rain
a light on my darkest days.

I drove to the airport to drop her off. As we hugged, I felt her needing me more than ever. I guided her about her job, goals, dreams, and the importance of waiting a couple of years before getting married. I tried my best to offer comfort and support, but deep down, I knew that the pain in my heart was resurfacing, the same pain that I had felt when Siya left. Sewing those pieces back together felt daunting, and I never imagined I would have to do it again.

I did not realise
that I loved you
so much
when you were right
in front of my eyes
and when I understood my feelings,
you bid me goodbye.

Before going, she shook my hands. She whispered in my ears that I had been her best friend she did not know she needed. I started to move back, and suddenly, she pulled me back and hugged me tight for one last time.

At that moment, I promised her that I would always be by her side, no matter the future. It was the only reassurance I could offer, and I hoped it would provide her with some comfort during this challenging time.

But I had to be strong, for her and myself. And so, with a heavy heart, I let her go, praying that our paths would cross again and that fate would bring us back together once more.

Let the time freeze and hold each other tight
and whisper our love to the
stars for in this moment my love
we are nothing but infinite

Love,
Siddhartha.

17th July, 2021

Dear Diary,

It has almost been a week since Alia flew to Jordan, and I cannot reach her. Her Dubai number is not working, and I am left in the dark, not knowing what is happening at her house or if she will ever return.

If we were never meant to be, why did we meet at the crossroads of life?

With every call and message notification, my heart leaps, hoping it is her. But no. Each time, a little piece of me breaks. I pray she is safe, but I do not know if I will ever see her again. Regret gnaws at me for not expressing my love, my feelings for her, and the possibility of us.

Perhaps she was never meant to be in my destiny.

There is hope in my heart that you will turn up once again in my life. Till then, I will wait

and let the fate decide.

Love,
Siddhartha.

She was not in my fate,
and that is why
I loved her so much.

20th July, 2021

Dear diary,

As the days pass and my life moves forward, the looming application deadlines draw nearer. I have decided to travel to the USA to visit business schools in person, hoping to gather inspiration for my application essays. I sent a heartfelt message to Alia, uncertain if she will ever read it or if she will even come back.

Despite this exciting opportunity to reach my dream, I cannot shake this overwhelming sadness. I should be thrilled, but my heart feels heavy, like I am leaving behind a piece of it. I cannot help but remember Alia with every step I take, and it pains me to think that she might not be a part of my future.

Mornings scare me
evenings depress
me even more
they say,

love bring butterflies
but here I am all
crestfallen and torn.

So many times, I feel the urge to send her a message telling in detail what she meant to me, and you would ask me why I never sent it.

Love,
Siddhartha.

The biggest puzzle
that I play in my mind
"What if she says no
and
what if she does not?"

I want to live in a world
that is not black and white
I want to breathe in a world
where you are by my side

30th July, 2021

Dear diary,

Amidst the vibrant tapestry of New York City, I found myself drawn to the hallowed halls of NYU, Yale, Cornell, and Columbia. These institutions, bastions of academic excellence, stood as beacons of hope, whispering tales of dreams nurtured and knowledge cultivated. From the bustling streets of Greenwich Village to the scholarly havens of New Haven and Ithaca, each corner exuded an aura of intellectual growth and boundless opportunity.

As I wandered through these esteemed institutions, the ghosts of generations whispered their stories, inspiring me to reach for the stars. The allure of these iconic towers, set against the backdrop of the city that never sleeps, ignited a fiery passion within me, propelling my ambitions to reach the uncharted heights.

Yet, amidst this whirlwind of excitement, a pang of longing tugged at my heartstrings. Alia's radiant smile and infectious laughter had left an indelible mark on my soul. As I strolled along the Brooklyn Bridge, witnessing couples lost in their worlds, the emptiness within me grew more palpable.

Tears welled in my eyes, a silent testament to the turmoil within. I should have been basking in the glow of my achievements, yet a part of me felt devoid of life. The uncertainty of Alia's fate gnawed at me, her silence a haunting reminder of the distance that had grown between us.

All I wished for was her happiness, regardless of the path life had chosen for us. I yearned to see her smile again, to hear her laughter fill the air. But for now, I was left with memories and unanswered questions, adrift in a sea of longing.

This emotional storm raged within me, disrupting raw, unfiltered expressions. I sought solace in your pages, hoping to find a semblance of calm amidst the chaos. Perhaps fate would reunite us one day, weaving our paths together again. Until then, I could only wish her well from afar, my heart yearning for the day our paths would intertwine again.

Walking across the bridge
moonlight spreading its wings
across the path
I saw a shiny shooting star
and all I could think about was you
even with miles of distance apart

Love,
Siddhartha.

2nd August, 2021

Dear diary,

Today, I hiked to see the iconic Hollywood sign. The glitz and glamour of this city feels straight out of a movie, yet even more enchanting. I visited the well-known USC Marshall campus. I want to be a poet one day, and Los Angeles can offer me abundant opportunities to grow and become a renowned artist.

I explored every corner of LA, from the Walk of Fame to Downtown's bustling streets and Hollywood's allure. Each step brought me closer to the heart of this vibrant city. As I set foot on the USC campus, I met various students from different countries. I inquired about poetry club, art shows, and whatnot. If I get into USC, it will be a dream come true for me.

Connecting the dots, Alexandria entered the scene. She is a remarkable individual, heading the student clubs and overseeing the vibrant art community at USC. In our conversations, she shared invaluable insights about the thriving poetry scene in LA and on campus. Her words ignited a spark in me, illustrating how USC could be the ideal launchpad for my dual passion: Business and the Arts. Alexandria's revelations about the poetry events in the city and the campus underscored the potential for me to flourish as a poet and an author.

Standing at the crossroads of ambition and opportunity, I envision USC as the perfect nexus of academic excellence and artistic growth. My aspirations of being a successful poet and author are seamlessly intertwined with the potential of USC's business programme, painting a vivid picture of a future where both dreams and pragmatic goals harmoniously coexist.

And now, let me share the most exhilarating news, diary. Alia messaged me! She is back in Dubai! We had a call, and I cannot describe the overwhelming happiness that washed over me when her name flashed on my mobile screen. Her number was not working in Jordan, and she could not use her parents' number to reach out, given their traditional ways.

But the moment she landed in Dubai, she called me. And even though it was midnight here, I woke up at the first ring. Oh, diary, the joy I felt at that moment was indescribable. She missed me too!

In this sea of dreams, my heart soars with hope and love.

Love,
Siddhartha.

No matter how far
I go,
my stupid heart
cannot stop
thinking about you.

4th August, 2021

Dear diary,

Today, I stepped into Harvard University, and it was a dream come true. The historic buildings, the vibrant atmosphere, and the energy of young, ambitious minds ignited a fire in my stomach. I could not help but feel overwhelmed by the possibilities that lay ahead.

As I wandered through the campus, my heart could not help but ache for Alia. I called her and showed her around through the video call. She was glad for me, but deep down, I wished she was beside me. I envisioned us exploring the campus together, making memories to cherish forever.

As I explored, another opportunity beckoned—MIT Sloan. Visiting their prestigious campus further fuelled my excitement and aspirations. The combination of intellect and innovation that permeated the air resonated deeply within me, igniting a fresh surge of determination.

With its serene charm and modern allure, Boston feels like a place straight out of a fairytale. Each street is adorned with its story, and I longed to share this enchanting city with Alia. From the historic Freedom Trail to the bustling Quincy Market, every corner held the potential for new adventures, and I could not help but miss her company.

Even amidst the excitement and beauty of Boston, there is an Alia-shaped gap within me. Our dreams are intertwined, and I wish for the day when we could explore the world together, hand in hand.

But until that day comes, I will embrace each moment, cherishing the experiences and leaving a piece of my heart in every place I visit, knowing that one day, I will return with Alia by my side.

Love,
Siddhartha.

My eyes
search for you
and hope you will appear
within the crowd
I hope you would
just whisper my name
and I will find your soul
from your distant sound

12th August, 2021

Dear diary,

Time seems to stretch like an eternity here in the USA, away from my love. On one hand, there are my dreams, and on the other, there is the yearning for the one who holds my heart, unaware of the depth of my feelings. The excitement to see her is overwhelming. Almost a month has passed since our last meeting, and I ache to gaze upon her face again.

Amidst countless people and fresh faces, I constantly searched for her presence. Amidst the excitement of exploring novel places, I felt a void within me, incomplete without her by my side. Every day, I can't help but imagine how perfect life would be if she were with me.

The time has come for me to board my flight, and I can hardly wait to be reunited with Alia. With each passing moment, my heart beats with anticipation, longing to hold her close and share all my experiences from this journey.

I will talk to you again, dear diary, once I am back in Dubai. With my heart full of love and cherished memories to share.

Heart was melting
jumping out of the skin
unexplainable happiness
coming from within.

Love,
Siddhartha.

I wish to
make you mine
if I find you
this time.

15th August, 2021

Dear diary,

Fate smiled upon me the moment I stepped foot in Dubai, for Alia called me. I knew she was waiting for me at the airport, and my heart raced excitedly. I hurried through security and immigration, eager to meet her as fast as possible.

As I emerged from the airport, she stood adorned in a red top and jeans. It is hard to put into words, but the sight of her felt like violins were playing, butterflies were soaring, and everything around us was fading into a blur. My focus was solely on her, and without a second thought, I ran towards her.

The moment I had dreamt of for days had finally arrived. She was just six feet away and instantly ran towards me, too. It was surreal, and I could hardly believe it was happening. And then she was in my arms, and my heart was pounding like never before.

But then, as she nestled in my embrace, I sensed her tears. Instinctively, I wiped them away, and that's when reality hit us both. The closeness and the vulnerability at that moment made us both feel awkward. But in that moment, I knew deep down that she had missed me too.

The feelings between us, unspoken yet palpable, held a promise of something magical.

In the flash of a second
I saw a million seasons
in your eyes
from sadness
to despair
to anger
to a happy high.

She spoke continuously on our way back to the hotel and did not let me speak. We sat on the rooftop until 3 a.m., and I had just returned. It feels like a dream, a dream which I hope never ends.

Love,
Siddhartha.

20th August, 2021

Let the time freeze
as we hold
each other tight
and whisper
our love to the stars
for in this moment,
we are nothing but infinite.

Dear diary,

Apologies for my absence. The applications have been consuming my time, leaving little space for penning my thoughts. But amidst the hustle, something extraordinary happened. Alia and I embarked on a long journey that unfolded new dimensions in our connection. As we cruised through the roads, I could not resist inquiring about her trip to Jordan, eager to share every detail of my adventure in the USA. Our bond grew more robust, and I opened up to her in ways I never had.

She also revealed something that touched my heart profoundly—she prays for me daily. It is a gesture transcending mere affection; it is a love that goes beyond the ordinary. In her prayers, I see her heart. It is a place where I feel cherished and cared for, like only my mother ever did.

The days have been filled with my full-time job and the pressure of applications; but just five minutes of conversation with Alia revitalises me, makes me forget the exhaustion, and helps me regain my focus on dreams. She is my source of motivation, the bright spark that keeps me going in this pursuit of greatness.

And as I look back on how far I have come, I cannot help but feel proud of myself. This journey has been challenging, but I have managed it with resilience and determination. I am on the verge of realising my dreams and cannot wait to see what the future holds.

With Alia by my side and the strength within me, I know I will conquer the world.

Love,
Siddhartha.

We could speak
even when we were silent,
and I knew we were in love.

20th September, 2021

Dear diary,

It has been two months since Alia broke up, but the memories of her past still haunt her. Today, I was in the office and got a call from her around 4 p.m. Generally, she does not call me during office hours. I hurriedly picked up to see if she was okay. As we spoke, I sensed that she was crying. I asked her to share her location with me as she was not at the hotel. I left my office and drove to the location. She was at Kite beach. I parked my car and ran towards her. She was sitting there all alone, looking at the shore.

Her eyes were deep in sadness, immersed in a world unknown to me.

I shrugged her to bring them back to their senses. On seeing me, she smiled but did not say anything. I sat next to her, trying to understand what she was going through. We sat there for a few hours without speaking anything.

On our way back in the car, she started speaking. I wanted her to let go of the pain that I could sense in her voice. While speaking, she started crying, and with each tear, she was letting go of her pain. I parked the car near the hotel and took her hand in mine. I just wanted to make her feel safe, heard, and know that I would always be there.

In the next few seconds, she hugged me. The warmth of her hug was touched my soul, as if she wanted me to hold her forever. I told her to let go of her pain, tears, and fears.

Suddenly, she whispered, "What if I can never love again? I feel scared."

I knew this feeling; I knew this pain. I also felt the same when Siya left me. I had never imagined I would ever be able to love someone again, but here I was, in love with Alia. But I did not have the nerve to tell her that, so I said nothing. I knew this was a phase, and she had to endure it, to escape it.

After a few minutes, she came out of my embrace, looked at me straight into my eyes, and said, "Thank you. Thank you for being with me in this tough time." I did not say a word. And just like that, she left me in the darkness, and I did not stop her. I knew that she would return to her room and cry her eyes out, but that was what was needed.

Love,
Siddhartha.

Shed me a tear,
cry me a river,
let go of your heartache,
do not think loving again
will be a yet new mistake
give love a chance,
for your sake

22nd September, 2021

Dear diary,

It has been a while since we had a heart-to-heart, so let me catch you up on the events sweeping through my life lately. Get ready, because it has been quite a crazy journey.

So here is the scoop—Alia made a new friend at her office, Zaheer, from Istanbul. They both are Arabs and share common interests. I am all for making friends, but this Zaheer guy took it to the next level. He decided that it was okay to bombard Alia's phone with messages even after work hours. At first, she tried being polite in her responses, but guess what? He escalated things from friendly chats to a whole-blown romantic proposal. I kid you not.

You can imagine the steam coming out from my ears when Alia told me about this. Seriously, how could he waltz in and propose to my Alia? It took all my willpower not to storm over there and give him a piece of my mind. Alia confronted him at the office, and let me tell you, he did not take it lightly. He started spreading rumours that they were having an affair, trying to pull her into the drama. But our girl Alia is made of solid stuff and decided to rise above the nonsense.

Fast forward to today, and I am in the middle of a real-life soap opera. I went to pick up Alia from her office, and guess what? No response to my calls. I waited in the basement for an eternity, growing more anxious by the second. Finally, I went up to the reception, and there she was, surrounded by a crowd, with Zaheer right smack in the centre. My heart raced as I hurried to her side, and she wrapped her arms around me like a lifeline.

Alia spilled the beans about the whole situation. It turned out this Zaheer had gone entirely relentless. He followed her into the elevator, got uncomfortably close, and pressurised her to say yes to his proposal. I could not hold back my anger any longer and gave him a good slap. But guess what? He did not take it lying down. He retaliated with punches and kicks, and we ended up in a brawl until others stepped in to break it up. He kept taunting Alia, and I could not just stand there. And in the heat of the moment, I blurted out that we were engaged and getting married in a month. He was shocked when listening to this, and I simultaneously felt happy and afraid.

Things got even crazier—security stepped in, and we were threatened with being taken to the police. I was ready to tear him apart, but Alia managed to pull me away, and we left the chaos behind. On our way, I let out my frustration on her, wondering why she had not told her manager earlier. She explained that it would have only added to the drama and gossip. She showed me his messages on her phone, reflecting how she had not encouraged his advances.

We cut off Zaheer's access by getting a new SIM card. It was a small step, but it did bring some relief. I told Alia to talk to her manager about it the next day itself to end the mess. But you know what? It was tough shaking off the anger and jealousy that had taken over me. I could not wrap my head around how someone could mess with what Alia and I have.

We hit McDonald's for ice cream sundaes to lighten the mood. Slowly, Alia's teasing managed to crack through the tension. But even so, my heart still felt jealous whenever she chatted with someone else. It is tough pretending that we are just pals, when my heart wants something more.

Diary, I cannot wait for the day when Alia becomes my partner for life. That day, I will proudly stand beside her and shout to the world that she is mine. Until then, I will be waiting impatiently, fuelled by a passionate longing. I am crossing my fingers that the universe plays its part, aligning the stars in our favour so that Alia finally comprehends how much she means to me.

Love,
Siddhartha.

24th September, 2021

Dear diary,

Today's entry is brimming with exciting news—interview calls from five renowned business schools have come pouring in! The whirlwind of preparations has begun, and guess who has taken up the role of my interview prep partner? None other than Alia herself.

Something was different today. A certain subtlety hung in the air, and after some gentle nudging, the truth spilled out. Alia had been pondering about the future once I move to the USA. What started as a light-hearted conversation, surprisingly took a severe turn.

With a playful wink, I threw her a wild idea. "How about you come to the States, and we'll live happily ever after?" To my astonishment, she ran with it.

"One day, after you get in the business school, we'll pack our bags and escape to the USA," she said.

"Sounds like a solid plan," I replied.

"But what about life there? How will we manage?" Alia wondered aloud.

"No worries, I'll work part-time, and my savings will cover us. Everything is sorted," I reassured her.

She grinned mischievously, "I've got a plan too. A pasta shop!"

"You mean 'Alia's Pasta'?" I teased.

"Exactly! And you will be the number one customer," she proclaimed.

"Of course, I'll practically live on Alia's Pasta," I laughed.

"But let's not get a huge house, just a cozy one," she proposed.

I played the devil's advocate, "Why not something grand?"

Her eyes sparkled, "We'll only be two people; we don't need extravagance. Happiness matters more."

"Okay, okay. Cozy it is," I surrendered.

As the sun dipped below the horizon, our light-hearted banter continued for hours, and before we knew it, the day had melted away. It is hard not to hope that our whimsical dreams might one day become our reality. I am left with a vivid image of a tiny home, a place where our shared dreams can find their roots.

Love,
Siddhartha.

25th September, 2021

Dear diary,

Life's been a cascade of excitement lately, and I have been diving headfirst into making friends in the USA while exploring various business school campuses. You remember the girl Alexandria, who was studying at USC Marshall? We connected instantly, and I got her number to take guidance for my USC interview. Alexandria is deeply involved in student clubs, which only adds to the allure of her insights.

So, picture this—Alia and I were perched on a rooftop, and I could not resist expressing my admiration for Alexandria. Just as I was animatedly narrating, ping! Alexandria messaged me. A smile tugged at my lips, anticipation dancing in my eyes. I mean, here was someone who could potentially hand me the keys to unlocking future opportunities. And then, I noticed something. Alia's expression shifted, a smirk playing on her lips.

Oh, the delightful twist! There it was, unmistakably, a hint of jealousy in Alia's eyes. I will admit that a rush of happiness coursed through me. I decided to ride the wave, embracing the playful drama that unfolded. I took the video call immediately, ensuring Alia was right there with me as I chatted with Alexandria. We laughed, sometimes at the silliest things, and I could feel Alia's intrigue growing.

Alia was on fire once the call wrapped up, peppering me with questions about Alexandria and finding trivial matters to bicker about. I could not resist poking fun at Alia a little, but eventually, I figured that it was not worth my time to indulge her this way.

Our conversation shifted gears, and beneath the moon's watchful gaze, we delved into the practical details of my applications, interview preps, and all that lay ahead. Ah, but duty calls, diary. Applications will need more time to finish themselves. Until next time.

Love,
Siddhartha.

I could uncover
the jealousy
and love that
you are trying to hide
deep in your eyes.

She was a moment
meant for a lifetime.

30th September, 2021

Dear diary,

Sorry for not writing for a few days, I was busy with my full-time job and MBA applications. So much happened since the last night. I told you about Alexandria in my previous entry, and guess what? She visited Dubai for an international trip with a few MBA classmates. She messaged me to see if we could meet. I was so happy to hear this. I told Alia to accompany me, and after much persuasion, she came with me to meet Alexandria and her friends.

We meet them in a bar. Alia does not drink, but I am a social drinker, so I thought I would drink with everyone. The excitement of seeing Alexandria after so long made me forget about everyone else, as we immersed ourselves in a lively chit-chat.

Meanwhile, Alia conversed with a few of her friends, but my attention kept gravitating towards her, ensuring she was comfortable and enjoying herself.

As the evening progressed, drinks flowed, and Alexandria's spirit soared to new heights. She asked me to dance with her, and though I agreed, I could not help but notice how Alia's demeanour shifted. She was visibly upset, and I was taken aback to witness this side of her for the first time. The fluttering sensation in my stomach was mixed with intrigue and fascination, and I found myself strangely drawn to this new facet of Alia.

Amidst the dancing and laughter, I noticed Alia leaving the bar abruptly. My instincts kicked in, and without hesitation, I excused myself from Alexandria's company and hurried after Alia. I called out her name, but she seemed determined to leave. The darkness of the night only added to the urgency as she walked briskly down the road. I called out her name again, and this time, she stopped.

What was it that had stirred such a strong reaction within her? I could not help but feel a tug at my heartstrings as I stood there, longing to know what lay beneath her unexpected response.

"Why are you leaving the bar?" I questioned, watching as Alia began to make her exit.

"None of your business. You go and enjoy with your girlfriend," she retorted, her tone tinged with annoyance and indifference.

"She's not my girlfriend," I clarified, the truth echoing in the space between us.

"Yes, she is. I noticed how closely you were dancing with her," Alia stated, her gaze unwavering.

"Are you jealous?" I could not help but inquire, my curiosity piqued.

"Why would I be jealous? Go. Get lost with her," she snapped back, her defences intact.

"I don't know," I admitted, a hint of mischief in my response.

"Stop assuming. I do not care about you," Alia declared, brushing off the topic as if it were inconsequential.

Jealousy was in the air.

As if her eyes were shouting at me
to look away
else she would fall in love with me

"All right. Then why are you leaving?" I inquired.

"I don't feel like staying there. Hence, I am leaving," she stated flatly.

"Oh. Okay," I assented, watching her take a few steps away. However, a sudden determination came to me, and I rushed after her. My hand reached out, grasping hers as I pulled her closer in the dimly-lit surroundings, bathed in the moon's gentle glow.

"You want to say something," I softly prompted, feeling the weight of unspoken words between us.

"No," she replied, her voice faint and hesitant.

"Yes, you do," I insisted, recognising the turmoil within her that mirrored my own.

"You should understand on your own," Alia countered, her walls still up.

"But I want to hear from you," I persisted, wanting to break through her defences.

"I hate you. You know that I like you, right?" she exclaimed, her emotions laid bare.

"Just like?" I questioned, delving deeper into her confession.

"Yes," Alia affirmed, her vulnerability evident.

"Are you sure?" I probed gently, seeking validation.

"Yes, I just like you. And I was jealous when I saw you with her," she admitted, revealing the undercurrents of her heart.

"Why? If you like me, why were you jealous?" I inquired, intrigued by the complexity of her words.

"Don't act smart. You know that I am in love with you," Alia finally bared her soul, the truth hanging in the air.

"You do," I acknowledged, feeling the weight of her revelation.

"Yes, I do. I love you so much. And I am jealous of her. And you can see that," she confessed, her words ringing authentically.

"Yes, I know. Are you not scared of love now?" I questioned, curious about her perspective.

"No, I am not. Because I'm in love with you. I feel at home with you, and that is enough for me," Alia shared, her sincerity undeniable.

"I love you too, Alia. I love you so much that words fall short," I finally confessed, the truth flowing freely between us.

This love that we share is both exhilarating and terrifying. We both know there are obstacles in our path, but our connection is undeniable. As I write, I cannot help but wonder what the future holds for us. Will we find a way to be together, or will circumstances keep us apart?

One thing is for sure. Alia has my heart, and I cannot imagine a life without her. I will cherish this moment forever, and no matter what happens, I promise to love her with all my heart, even if we do not end up together. Our love may be complicated, but it is worth every moment of joy and pain.

Love,
Siddhartha.

01st October, 2021

I craved for intimacy
but she touched my soul,
and she was all I ever needed.

Dear diary,

Today, I officially asked Alia out on a date. The feeling was quite different, as until yesterday we were just friends, and now she was going to be my girlfriend.

She told me to pick her up tomorrow evening at seven, and I could not stop smiling. The excitement was bubbling inside me, and I could not wait to spend time with her. I tried to hide my giddiness, afraid she might find me too eager, but deep inside, I was jumping joyfully. As she left the rooftop, she turned back and playfully reminded me not to be late. Her laughter filled the air, and I could not help but feel even more drawn to her. I waved her goodbye, and she disappeared from my sight, but not from my thoughts.

I have spent hours planning the perfect date for her. I want to make sure she has a memorable time with me. After much thought, I took her to Al Seef, an enchanting open-night Arabic market. The atmosphere there is captivating, just like her, and I know she would love it.

I lay in bed, unable to sleep, my mind racing with excitement and nerves. I have replayed our conversations and have imagined how the evening would unfold. Every minute feels like an eternity, but I know it would be worth the wait.

I cannot wait for tomorrow to come, when I see her again and embark on this journey together. My heart is overflowing, and I cannot help but hope that this date will mark the beginning of something beautiful between us.

Love,
Siddhartha.

Are you as excited as I am?
because I cannot wait
to see you again.

2nd October, 2021

Her soul collided with mine
and no one else will be enough
in this lifetime.

Dear diary,

Tonight was a fairy tale. Alia looked radiant, and her smile outshone the lights in the bustling night market. Our hands accidentally touched as we walked by my side, and an electrifying jolt shot through me. I could not resist the urge to hold her hand in mine, and to my surprise, she did not pull away. It was as if time stood still in that moment, and I never wanted to let go of that feeling.

Trying to play it cool, pretend that it was all casual, but Alia saw right through me and burst into laughter. I too joined in, my heart fluttering with joy at her laughter. And then, without any hesitation, she came closer and took my hands in hers, confirming what I had hoped for—we were a couple now.

The evening was filled with laughter, conversations, and a stronger connection with every passing moment. I could not have asked for a more perfect date. We ended up in a cozy cafe for coffee, and then proceeded to a romantic dinner. The chemistry between us was undeniable, and I fell for her with every word she spoke.

On our way back, we did not feel the need to fill the silence with words. The silence was but an unspoken understanding of what we felt. It was a moment of pure bliss, and I wanted to hold onto it forever.

I knew it was time to say goodnight as we reached her hotel. I could not let her go without expressing how much she meant to me, so I took her hand and kissed it gently. The blush on her cheeks made my heart skip a beat. With a shy smile, she ran inside, and I watched her until she disappeared from my sight.

I cannot believe how lucky I am to have her. Tonight, in her eyes, I saw what I had been feeling in my heart all along—we were meant to be together. I cannot wait to see what the future holds for us, and I am confident that this is just the beginning of a beautiful love story.

Love,
Siddhartha.

I loved her
without a reason
and that was the only
reason that I loved her.

05th October, 2021

Dear diary,

Tonight was a chapter written in the stars, a tale of enchantment spun against Dubai's sparkling skyline. The air was filled with an electrifying anticipation as we embarked on a journey that would forever etch itself in my heart.

The evening began with a soft breeze that carried the promise of something magical. Alia's smile illuminated the darkness as we stepped out onto the streets. Her eyes held a glimmer of excitement, a spark that mirrored the city's dazzling lights. We strolled, our footsteps echoing off of the bustling streets, while my heartbeat was in rhythm with the city's pulse.

The sights and sounds of Dubai surrounded us, but Alia held my attention. Her laughter was music to my ears, a melody that blended seamlessly with the city's vibrant energy. With every passing moment, the world faded, and it was just the two of us—lost in our own world.

As we walked, our conversations flowed effortlessly, as if we had known each other forever. Her stories painted vivid images in my mind, and I found myself hanging onto her every word. We spoke of dreams, aspirations, and the endless possibilities that lay stretched before us.

The pièce de résistance of the evening was when we found ourselves on a secluded balcony overlooking the city's lights. The skyline seemed to dance in celebration of our newfound connection. The night sky, adorned with stars, mirrored the twinkle in Alia's eyes. We sat there, our hearts open like the city beneath us, basking in the glow of each other's company. And then, in a moment that almost took my breath away, Alia's hand found mine again. Our fingers intertwined, the touch igniting a smouldering fire since we had met.

We gazed at the stars, hand in hand, sharing whispered promises and dreams. The world around us felt distant and irrelevant—the connection between our intertwined fingers held all the meaning.

As the night passed, we reluctantly returned to the bustling streets below. Our fingers remained entwined, a silent testament to the bond between us. And though our evening in Dubai had ended, the memories we created would forever be etched into the fabric of our story.

With every step we took back to reality, my heart held onto the magic of our shared moments. The city had witnessed a romance unfolding, a chapter written in the stars—a chapter I shall cherish for all eternity.

Love,
Siddhartha.

Hand in hand,
we roamed
to create a love
that we can call our own.

We danced
amidst the city's art,
and in that moment,
I knew, she held my heart.

20th October, 2021

Dear diary,

Tonight, the universe whispered the secrets of love as I celebrated Alia's birthday amidst the delights of Dubai. It was a symphony of surprises and a dance of hearts, as I orchestrated a magical evening for us.

The day began with a sun-kissed visit to the Atlantis, a paradise nestled amidst the azure waves. Alia's laughter echoed through the corridors as we explored its wonders hand in hand. Beneath the aqua glow of the aquarium, our eyes met—a silent promise of more wonders yet to come.

As the sun dipped below the horizon, we ventured into the heart of Dubai, its lights mirroring the twinkle in Alia's eyes. The city was alive with the energy of our shared anticipation. Little did she know, the night held secrets yet unrevealed.

A rooftop dinner awaited, a sea of candles and stars framing the night sky. Alia's surprised gasp was the sweetest melody as she saw the spread before us. We savoured the flavours of our love and shared dreams with every dish and every sip.

But the grandest surprise was yet to come. Anxiously, I led her to a private terrace where the Dubai Fountain danced to our song as if the world was celebrating her existence. Her eyes held mine, a reflection of the stars above, as the music swirled around us.

At that moment, as we swayed to the rhythm of our hearts, I knew that this was the beginning of a beautiful journey. It will be a journey of surprises, laughter, shared dreams, and a love that flourishes with every passing moment.

As the night ended, we found ourselves gazing at the stars, hands and our hearts entwined like constellations in the night sky. And in that embrace, I knew that Alia's birthday had become a chapter etched in the story of our love.

Love,
Siddhartha.

Sunkissed, star-gazed,
both of us
in an empty space
felt like a painting
on a canvas
but still the world
could not see us.

21st October, 2021

A promise I made,
a promise
you should keep,
even if my name is
not in your palm
you will always remember me.

Dear diary,

Today was both heartache and hope.

"I don't know what the future holds for us, Siddhartha," she said softly, her voice trembling. "But I want you to promise me something."

"What is it, Alia?" I asked, with my heart in my throat.

"Promise me that no matter what happens, where life takes us, we will always love each other," she said, locking her eyes with mine.

"I promise, Alia," I said, tears welling. "I will always love you, no matter what."

She reached out and held my hand, and I could feel the warmth of her touch seeping into my soul. "Even if we don't end

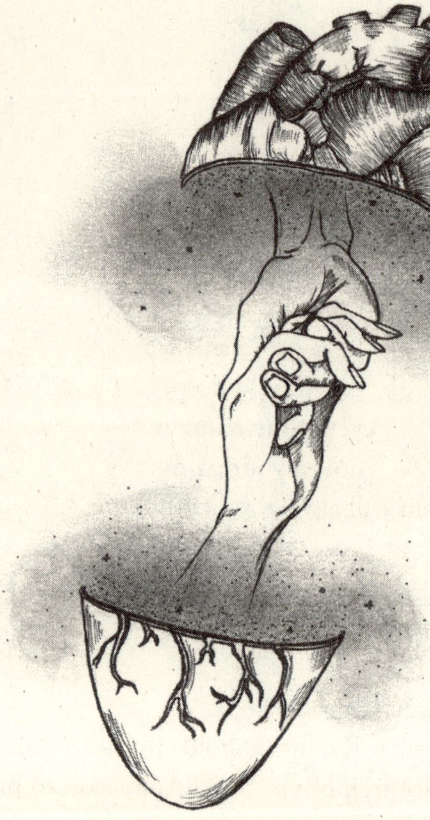

up together, even if we don't get married, promise me that we will always cherish the love we shared."

I nodded. My voice choked as I said, "I promise, Alia. Our love will always be a cherished memory in my heart."

As we stood there, holding each other's gaze, I knew that this promise was more than just words. It was a pact between two souls who had found something special in each other, something that transcended time and distance.

We would find each other
not because
you need me
or I am right
because we are soulmates shining
under the same twilight

Love,
Siddhartha.

05th December, 2021

Dear diary,

My heart is brimming with joy and excitement as I share an incredible news with you. I got into USC Marshall, my dream business school in Los Angeles! That too, with a great scholarship! I can hardly believe it, but it is true. I feel like the world is mine for taking.

As soon as I received the acceptance letter, I could not wait to share this news with Alia. She has been my constant support throughout this journey, and I knew that she would be thrilled. I rushed to call her, my heart pounding with anticipation.

When she picked up the phone, her voice exuded warmth. I could picture her beautiful smile on the other end of the line. "Alia, guess what? I got into USC Marshall! Can you believe it?" I exclaimed, unable to contain my excitement.

There was a brief pause before she replied, "Oh, my goodness, that's amazing! I am so proud of you! Congratulations!" Her genuine enthusiasm filled my heart with even more joy. "I couldn't have done it without your support, Alia. You have been my pillar of strength," I confessed, my voice tinged with gratitude.

Then, we began discussing everything from the upcoming adventure in Los Angeles to reminiscing about the past memories. The way she laughed at my silly jokes made me feel like the luckiest guy in the world.

But as the conversation progressed, a hint of hesitation crept into my mind. I could not help but wonder how my decision to move to Los Angeles would affect us. Our bond was undeniable, but the distance between us would soon be undeniable, too.

"Alia, there's something I want to talk to you about," I mustered the courage to bring up my concern.

"What is it, Sid?" she asked, sensing my change in tone.

"I got into USC Marshall, and it's my dream come true. But... it means that I will be moving to Los Angeles. I do not know how this will work for us," I confessed, my heart racing due to the uncertainly.

There was a moment of silence before she spoke, her voice calm yet filled with excitement.

"Sid, I'm really happy for you and want you to pursue your dreams. But I can't deny that being apart would make me anxious too."

My heart sank slightly at her response, but I understood her concern. "I don't want to lose you, Alia," I said, vulnerably.

"We've been through so much together, and I cherish every moment that we've shared," she replied softly. "But love isn't about holding someone back. If you truly want this and USC Marshall is the path towards your dreams, then I'll support you, Sid."

Her words touched me deeply, and I felt a surge of love and admiration for this incredible woman. "Thank you, Alia. Your support means everything to me."

"We'll figure it out. No matter what, we will always have each other," she reassured me, and I knew then, our love was resilient and capable of weathering any storm.

As I hung up the phone, a sense of determination filled me. USC Marshall might physically take me away from Alia, but our hearts will remain intertwined, no matter the distance. This was just the beginning of our story. I was ready to face the challenges that lay ahead as I pursued my dreams in Los Angeles, with Alia cheering me on.

Love,
Siddhartha.

What if our love story was
written
briefly in the sand
and time was not on our side and
perhaps that was
just the beginning of an end.

10th December, 2021

Dear diary,

Today, our story took an unexpected turn, a twist that has left my heart in turmoil. Alia confided in her sister about our love, trusting her to keep it a secret. But the trust was misplaced, as her sister shared our secret with their father.

The phone call came as a shock. Alia's father's voice was angry and disappointed, his words sharp and cutting. He disapproved of our relationship, and his concerns rooted in our differing backgrounds and beliefs. The clash was palpable, like a storm brewing within the confines of a phone call.

As Alia listened, her face shifted from surprise to a mixture of sorrow and frustration. Her father's words were like a gulf widening between us, a gulf formed by traditions and cultural differences. The love that once felt invincible, now stood at the mercy of a disapproving gaze. My heart ached as I held Alia's hand, our connection resembling a lifeline amidst the tumult. It was as if a wall had suddenly risen, blocking the path we had walked on together so far. The turmoil in her eyes mirrored the turmoil within me.

As the phone call ended, a cloud of uncertainty appeared. Our love story, once a tapestry woven with hope and dreams, now faced a challenge it had not foreseen. Alia's father's disapproval had casted a shadow over our path, leaving us at a crossroads.

During this storm, I am resolved to stand by Alia's side to navigate the challenges ahead together. Our love might be facing its most arduous trial yet, but the strength of our connection can overcome even the most rigid of barriers.

Love,
Siddhartha.

What if
there are no tomorrows,
what if the future, if any
holds just sorrows,
what if our love
remains just
an incomplete rhyme
and we were just
fleeting moments
all this while?

14th December, 2021

Dear diary,

Tonight, under the canopy of stars, I took a leap of faith, baring my heart to Alia in a way I had never before. I proposed my words to her, promising eternal love and a plea for us to embrace the unknown together.

I poured my heart out as I gazed into her eyes, illuminated by the moon's gentle glow. I confessed my unwavering love and painted a picture of a future where we would be bound by our shared dreams, not constrained by the shackles of tradition.

I asked her to run away with me, to leave behind the shadows of disapproval and embrace the light of our love. I wanted to whisk her away to a world where our hearts could sing freely, where we could author our own stories without the limitations set by her father's beliefs. But her answer was a heartbreaking whisper of fear, a glimpse into the cage that tradition and familial expectations had created. She shook her head, her eyes glistening with unshed tears. She confessed her love and her dreams of a life with me, but the weight of her father's disapproval held her captive.

In that moment, my heart shattered. It was as if our love, a flame that burned so brightly within us, was doused by the icy waters of fear and tradition. As she apologised and backed away, a chasm opened between us, which felt insurmountable.

I watched her walk away, my heart heavy with a mix of sorrow and determination. The battle between our love and the constraints of tradition had reached its zenith, and in that moment, tradition seemed to have won.

Yet, as I stood amidst the night's silence, I knew my love for Alia would never waver. Our journey might have taken a heart-wrenching turn, but I was resolved to find a way to bridge that chasm, and show Alia that love can conquer even the most formidable of obstacles.

Love,
Siddhartha.

I want
all my tomorrows,
all my nights
with you
because
I can never love anyone
more than I do love you.

15th December, 2021

Dear diary,

Amidst the storm that has shaken my world, I sought refuge in the one person whose wisdom and love have always been my anchor—my mother. I dialled her number with a heavy heart, longing for her counsel and understanding.

I felt a familiar sense of comfort as her voice flowed through the phone. She listened intently as I poured my heart out, explaining the complexities pulling me apart. I sensed her empathy with every word she spoke, as if she could feel my pain as deeply as I did.

When I finally finished, there was a pause. A silence that seemed to bridge the distance between us. Then, in a calm and measured tone that only a mother possesses, she began to speak. She acknowledged my pain, the choices I was faced with, and the love that tugged at my heart.

But she also spoke of the importance of following my dreams, of not letting the fire of ambition be extinguished by circumstances. Her words carried the wisdom of years and the weight of experience, a reminder that life often presents us with challenges that evaluate our resolve and reshape our paths.

As she explained her perspective, I felt different emotions arise within me—the agony of leaving behind a love woven into my being and the yearning to pursue the dreams that had driven me for so long. Her logic was clear, her advice sound, yet my turmoil remained.

Then, as our conversation neared the end, she offered a glimmer of hope. She told me that she understood the depth of my love and that love sometimes requires sacrifices. But she also offered to talk to Alia's parents to bridge the gap of tradition and differences.

Her offer was like a ray of light piercing through the darkness. In her voice, I could hear the love of a mother and the strength and resilience that had carried her through life's challenges. It was a reminder that love can be a bridge, and sometimes, family can be the force that helps us overcome the barriers that seem impossible.

As I hung up the phone, I was left with gratitude for my mother's unwavering support and a glimmer of hope. The hope that a solution could still be found amidst the chaos. The road ahead is still uncertain, but with my mother's love and guidance, I am determined to navigate it with courage and conviction.

Love,
Siddhartha.

One day,
If you wake up and
find me gone,
remember that I always loved you with all
my heart,
but I was too afraid of fighting
with my broken stars.

17th December, 2021

Dear diary,

The crossroads have grown even more complex, leaving us entangled in a web of love and ambition. Alia's plea for me to stay and help her bridge the gap with her father clashes with the call of my dreams, pulling me in opposite directions.

She stood before me, her eyes glistening with hope and desperation, and implored me not to leave for the USA. She believed that with time, through my unwavering presence by her side, she could persuade her father to accept our love. But my dreams have been years in the making, a foundation that I cannot abandon lightly.

Caught between love and ambition, I gazed into Alia's eyes, my heart heavy with the weight of our choices. Her request melted my heart, but the pull of my dreams is equally potent. The dilemma is a storm raging within me, one that I never foresaw.

As our silence hangs heavy in the air, I see the conflict mirrored in her eyes. We stand at the crossroads, our paths uncertain and diverging. It is as if the universe is testing our love's limits, pitting it against our individual aspirations.

During this turmoil, one thing is for sure—our love is resilient. Though the current circumstances might seem dire, love can inspire change and bridge the seemingly impossible gaps.

Our future remains uncertain, and our paths are fraught with challenges. But as I stand here, I am resolved to find a way to navigate this complexity. I want to show Alia that love does not just conquer obstacles—it can also pave new roads, leading to unimagined destinations.

Love,
Siddhartha.

22nd December, 2021

Dear diary,

Hopes and fears converged as I penned an email to the admission team of USC Marshall, seeking to defer my MBA for a year. With a heart full of longing, I explained the situation, hoping that fate would grant me this reprieve, allowing me to stay and bridge the chasm between my love for Alia and my dreams.

The team's response arrived days later, a digital harbinger of my heart's descent. The words were succinct yet heavy with finality. The deferral could not be granted as my reason was not a medical or threatening condition. And worse yet, if I applied next year, the chances of getting a scholarship seemed low. It was as if my dreams were slipping through my fingers, leaving only the residue of what might have been.

The implications unfurled like a tattered banner of reality. The loan I had availed of, other than the scholarship amount, the payment made towards the MBA, and the housing expenses, were now investments with uncertain returns. The financial burden weighed heavily, each expense a testament to my choices in pursuit of a future that now seemed out of reach.

And as if that were not enough, I found myself on a precipice at my current job. I had resigned, a step taken confidently for pursuing greater horizons. But with the MBA plans now dashed, I was left with a three-month notice period and an uncertain future.

Amid this turmoil, my dreams and ambitions clashed with the Alia-shaped ache in my heart. The dreams I had nurtured for years now had a companion—the vision of a life intertwined with the woman I loved. It was a tug of war between the life I had planned and the life my heart now yearned for.

My mother's face appeared before me; a portrait of strength forged through adversity. As a single parent, she had navigated the stormy seas of life, sacrificing her own dreams to provide for me. Her struggles were etched into her eyes, her determination a guiding light that had helped me reach for my aspirations. In my heart, I knew that my mother's sacrifices were not in vain. And while my situation was different, the choices before me echoed her past—having to choose between love and ambition, between dreams and the responsibilities that life placed upon us.

As I stared at the email, a sadness churned within me. The path ahead was uncertain, fraught with challenges I am yet to anticipate. Right now, I am just trying to figure out what to do and where to go.

Love,
Siddhartha.

We were sad,
just pretending
to be happy,
time became still
and our love
was fading eventually,
and no morphine
would ever be enough
to erase the memories.

22nd January, 2022

Dear diary,

Today, after a month of discussions, Alia and I went to The Atmosphere in Burj Khalifa to celebrate my success. We went to the 137th floor. I could see the entire Dubai from the hotel window and could not believe that I was literally at the top of the world's tallest building.

Flying among the clouds, floating amidst the stars, I held her hand. I never realised we had come this far.

We ordered a cake and celebrated. I could not believe my luck, I was celebrating this milestone with the love of my life. While immersing in the hotel's atmosphere, reality soon kicked in.

Alia could sense why I was sad, and she felt sadder. The vibe of the entire celebration changed—we both pretended to be happy, but deep in our hearts, we were not. We were scared about the future, but neither of us wanted to spoil the evening, so we pretended that it was all okay even though it was not.

Love,
Siddhartha.

Happiness is like a curse to me,
like the silence before the storm
waiting to blow everything away
whom I have once called my own.

25th January, 2022

Dear diary,

Will it hurt again? It always hurts, right? I don't know, but I must figure it out myself. Again. Honestly, I am scared. I am hell-scared because I know I love her, but I must pursue my dreams, and there is also so much uncertainty—our families, religion, cultural differences, time difference, distance, and whatnot.

I don't know how we will make it work, but do I know that I love her more than anyone I have ever loved. I do not want to live in a world where she is not mine. I do not want to breathe anymore if she is not the reason that I will be alive.

I think the time has come to face the world and our demons. I don't know what she will say, but if she loves me, she will also fight the world.

As I stand at the crossroads of life
I cannot help but realise
how far we have come my dear and
how far we still must travel

Will our love pass the test of life or will it
crumble under the pressure of culture,
differences, distance, and time?
Will it be able to steer and make it to the end or
we will end this and try to remain just friends.

Love,
Siddhartha.

27th January, 2022

Dear diary,

In the labyrinth of decisions to be taken, my mother has emerged as a beacon of hope, a force determined to bridge the chasm between love and reality. With courage in her heart, she took a daunting step—she called Alia's father.

The conversation was a testament of her unwavering love for me and her belief in the power of unity. She spoke sincerely, with a mother's hope that their shared love for Alia and me might help bridge the gap.

But the response was a sad gust of reality. Alia's father's words held the weight of disapproval, a resounding echo of what we had already feared. It was as if tradition and beliefs stood as insurmountable walls, separating us from the future we had dreamt of.

Yet, my mother's determination did not waver. Her next call was to Alia, a voice of solace and understanding amidst the storm. She conveyed her love and blessings with a tenderness that only a mother could provide. In that moment, Alia must have felt the warmth of a mother's embrace, a reminder that love can transcend even at the face of adversity.

Then came the call that carried the weight of the world. My mother's voice held a mixture of sadness and wisdom, a reminder of the dreams we had nurtured and the sacrifices she had made as a single parent. She understood my heart's yearning and the importance of my dreams—dreams that had been woven into my identity for years.

She spoke with the clarity of someone who had navigated life's challenges and had made tough choices to pave the way for the future. My future. And in that conversation, her voice embodied the love that had always guided me, a love that was willing to let go, if it meant my dreams would soar.

As I hung up the phone, a heavy silence enveloped me. The battle between love and ambition raged within me, a storm that refused to be quelled. It was a moment of reckoning, a choice that would determine the course of my life.

In the face of uncertainty, I held onto my mother's words and the love surrounding me. The path ahead might be unclear; but with her guidance and support, I am determined to choose the path that honours my dreams and the sacrifices that have shaped me into who I am today.

Love,
Siddhartha.

We were always
a losing game
yet, we played.
It was neither your fault
nor it was mine;
we were two perfect souls
who met in the wrong life.

25th March, 2022

Dear diary,

My heart was torn between my dreams and my love for Alia. As our conversations continued, silence settled like a heavy fog, and I could feel the weight of our words hanging in the air. She is correct, it will take work. But the distance, the time difference, the cultural differences—all seem like insurmountable obstacles.

But my dream of going to Los Angeles, to USC Marshall, has been a long-held aspiration. I had worked tirelessly for this opportunity and cannot let it slip away. At the same time, I cannot bear the thought of leaving Alia behind.

I asked her to elope and leave her family behind, as they would never approve of our love. But, I could sense her hesitance. I understood that she did not want to run away from her family. I did not want to pressure her into deciding when she was not ready for it, but the pain of leaving her behind was almost unbearable.

"I can't say the same thing again and again," she said, and her words pierced through me. You cannot leave your dream; I cannot leave my family. Then what do we do?

"I do not know. I do not know what to do, Alia," I said in the lowest voice I could muster.

In the face of challenges, we held each other close. I looked at her, and I could not hold back my tears. From what I thought we would have been to what we were—our mirage slowly disappeared and left nothing behind.

Ultimately, we parted with heavy hearts, both uncertain about what the future held for us. But deep down, I knew that my love for Alia will never fade, no matter where life takes us. I was willing to wait and see if fate would bring us back together, and if not, I would always cherish the memories of our time together.

Love,
Siddhartha.

There was silence as we spoke
and I could sense we were falling out of love.

Time was up and she wanted to leave
and I was no longer a reason for her to stay so, I
had to let her go.

30th March, 2022

Dear diary,

So, this was it, our last date together.

I had asked Alia to join me on a date, hoping to end our time together on a happy note despite the impending farewell. It was hard to fathom that this could be the end. That even after spending so many months together, our paths would diverge. But she agreed to come, and I could not help but feel a glimmer of hope in my heart. The same happiness that I felt when she agreed to our first date resurfaced, and for a moment, it felt like nothing had changed.

The plan was to take her on a short local cruise, to a special place where we could create more cherished memories. The day of our date arrived, and I could not shake the anxious feeling gnawing at me. It was as if I was losing something precious, and the fear of letting go was overwhelming.

I suddenly had the urge to hold her hand in the car, just like I always did whenever she got in. But this time, uncertainty held me back. What if she did not want that anymore? What if this gesture was too much for her now? So, I let the moment pass, feeling a pang of regret.

As we started our journey, I had brought along her favourite things—red flowers, chips, and chocolates. I remembered how her eyes used to light up at the sight of these little surprises. It was a small gesture, but I hoped it could make her smile.

I tried to uplift the mood by asking her to play her favourite songs which she loved dancing to, in the car. But to my surprise, she refused. It was unusual, and I knew what was bothering her. Despite my attempts to convince her, she remained adamant.

Instead, I turned on the FM, and as fate would have it, the song that played was "We Don't Talk Anymore". The irony was not lost, and I felt a lump in my throat. The lyrics echoed in my mind, resonating with our unspoken feelings.

Throughout the ride, she seemed lost in her thoughts, and I wished to know what was happening in her mind. We had shared so much with each other, and it was hard to believe this could be the end. But I had to cherish this moment, be present, and embrace whatever it brought.

Love,
Siddhartha.

Let me die because
I do not want such a life where I know
you exist
and I cannot call you mine.
So let me die!

01st April, 2022

Her eyes would take me to
the sea
where I had never been before
and the same eyes
made me cry
broke my heart into million pieces and
she yet was asking me, why?

Dear diary,

On the cruise, we took the seats atop. It felt so different, as I knew this would be my last time seeing her. After this night, we would part ways.

We started talking about old times, about us, about everything.

Alia's voice trembled with a mix of confusion and pain. "You told me once that we were soulmates. So why are you leaving me?"

I took a deep breath, my heart heavy with the weight of my decision. "I'm not leaving you. I asked you to come with me. But you have made it clear that you do not want to. Going to the USA and attending my dream school is an opportunity I cannot let slip away. This chance won't come again."

"So, you're okay with losing me?" Alia's voice quivered, the hurt palpable in her words.

"Our relationship has no future," I replied, a tinge of resignation in my tone. "Your parents won't approve. And realistically, you can't just run away with me."

"But I told you, I need some time to convince them," Alia pleaded, desperately.

"How much more time can I give?" I questioned, the urgency of my dream tugging at my heart. "I can't wait indefinitely. I can't sacrifice my dreams and get stuck here."

"Why can't we try a long-distance relationship while I work things out?" I suggested, with hope clinging on to my words.

"Because it won't work," she countered. "We'll be worlds apart, with a 12-hour time difference. Our lives will change, and the strain will lead to fights. Moreover, my father will seize the distance as an opportunity to marry me off to someone else."

"This is insane. Why did you fall in love with me when you knew this could never work? What am I supposed to do now?" I sighed, the pain of reality settling in. "I love you, Alia. But love alone is not enough. I can wait, but only if there is a guarantee they will agree. We must be practical. This is not a movie. We cannot chase a fantasy if it leads to unbearable pain in the end."

She could not hold back her tears. She was extremely sad. The eyes that used to twinkle when we met were sad for the first time, and I was the reason.

I hope that we can have a pleasant time together. Yet my mind cannot help but dwell on the many "what ifs" for which I have no answers. I decided to go with the flow, knowing that sometimes life's twists and turns take us to places we never expected.

Just whisper my name
for one last time
as if I feel lifeless
realising you can never be mine.

Love,
Siddhartha.

Just like the sea
you were enchanting,
but I was the shore
hence, we could never meet.

Let us meet again, maybe
at the right time
and we will tell what's in our minds, till
then, I will wait my love
even if it means finding you in my
next life.

02nd April, 2022

Dear diary,

The cruise was beautiful, but the shadow of our impending separation loomed over us. We tried to enjoy the scenery and the company, but it was bittersweet. The sun began to set, painting the sky in hues of orange and pink.

As we drove back, the atmosphere was heavy with unspoken words. I wanted to say so much, hold her close and tell her how much she meant to me, but I was afraid of the outcome. The fear of what might happen if I opened my heart ultimately held me back.

We reached her place, and the moment to say goodbye had come. I looked into her eyes, trying to convey all the love and memories we had shared without uttering a word. I could see the same emotions mirrored in her gaze.

Alia's voice trembled with uncertainty. "So, what do we do?"

I replied, my voice gentle yet heavy with resignation. "We leave our chapter unfinished. Maybe, just maybe, fate will bring us back together when the time is right, when we are not bound by constraints and running out of time. Until then, I'll wait for you."

Her voice quivered with hope, seeking reassurance. "You promise?"

"Till death tears us apart, I'll wait for you," I vowed, the conviction in my words unwavering.

"You won't forget me?" Alia's voice held a tinge of vulnerability.

"How can one forget one's soul? I love you, and that love will remain eternal." I assured her.

"Why isn't love enough?" she lamented, the pain evident in her question.

"It's a cruel truth, but it rarely is," I replied, my voice carrying the weight of the reality we were facing.

Her final question was charged with longing, "When will we meet again?"

I wished I had an answer, a glimpse into the future, but all I could do was offer a promise of hope. One day, I will find you there when the aqua seas meet the cloudy skies. Till next time, my love, till next time.

We hugged, and I knew it was time to let her go. We did not talk anymore, but our hearts carried a language of their own—one filled with love, shared memories, and the hope that someday, our paths might intertwine again. As she stepped out of the car, I wished for a moment that time could stand still.

She left, leaving behind our memories and incredible sadness. Our last date had ended, but the memories we created would forever be etched in my heart. Perhaps fate had different plans for us, but in that moment, I knew that what we had shared was exceptional, and it would live on as a cherished chapter in the story of our lives.

I stood there until she got inside. It was heartbreaking. I never thought this would hurt so badly. I turned back and started walking towards my car. Inside the car, I could still feel her presence. I could smell her fragrance. I do not know when I started crying.

The more I resisted, the more I cried.

I felt so lonely in that car. I drove back to the parking with teary eyes. And my heart told me: Maybe in the next life.

If we were never
meant to be
then why did
we meet
at the crossroads of life?

Love,
Siddhartha.

Maybe I wanted her to stay
and she wanted me to stop her,
but no one did anything
and just in a blink of an eye, forever yours
became a last goodbye.

05th April, 2022

Dear diary,

I am about to leave for the US in two days, but my heart feels heavy with sorrow. Today, I feel like the world is crumbling around me. We had to make the painful decision to part ways because there was no future for us, and it is tearing me apart.

As I reflect on our time together, I cannot help but replay all the beautiful memories in my mind. The laughter we shared, the late-night conversations that made the time fly, and the warmth of her touch—all these moments are etched into my heart, and I fear they will haunt me in the coming days.

But life is cruel, and sometimes love alone is not enough to conquer the obstacles that stand in our way. Our dreams led us down different paths, and we knew that holding on would only cause more pain eventually. It is the kind of pain that is so deep and consuming it leaves you breathless.

As I sit here, my eyes fill up with tears, and I struggle to hold them back. The pain of leaving Alia behind was unbearable, and I wondered if I would ever be whole again without her by my side. It is like a part of me is missing; I fear it will never be found.

I wish things were different, that our love could defy all odds and triumph over any obstacle. But reality is a harsh mistress, and she reminds us that sometimes we must let go of the things we love the most, even if it breaks us in the process.

I want to hold on to Alia, beg her to come with me, and fight for us against all odds. But deep down, I know that it is not fair to her, and it is not fair to myself. We both deserve a chance to find happiness, even if it means we must do it apart.

I went to Alia's house today to give her this diary, but she did not take it and sent me away. So, I went to Aditya's place. I requested him to deliver it to her once I was gone to the USA. And maybe by then, Alia would have calmed down. This will be my last chapter, and I hope you have also felt what I did, throughout my journey.

As I prepare for a new journey, my heart feels heavy with grief, and I cannot help but wonder if I will ever see Alia again. It feels like I am losing a part of myself, and I am terrified of what the future holds without her in it.

But as painful as this moment is, I know I must be strong. I must believe that one day, the ache in my heart will ease, and I will find happiness again. Until then, I will carry the memories of our love with me, cherishing them like precious treasures.

Love,
Siddhartha.

Entrapped in a whirlwind
you are circling around,
please lend me a helping hand
because I am hating this painful sound

The Present

4

Alia

Alia's trembling voice pierced through the line. "Hello Aditya, this is Alia. I read Siddhartha's diary. I saw myself through his eyes. I never ever knew that he loved me so much. I never knew that he was battling with depression, OCD, and loneliness. And despite it all, he was fighting for his dream alone. I feel so sad that I did not support him enough. I never fully realised how important this dream was to him."

Relief was palpable in Aditya's response, "Oh, so you finally read the diary. Thank goodness."

Alia's urgency grew. "Where is Sid? Why did he ask you to give me this diary? He never mentioned speaking with USC's admissions team for a deferral. He never told me anything. He loved me from the very beginning. He kept everything hidden. I feel devastated. I need to talk to him. I cannot believe that I thought he abandoned us for his dreams without a second thought. I had no idea he fought so hard."

Aditya's explanation was laden with regret, "Before he left for the airport, he came to give you the diary himself, but you didn't accept it."

"I was angry," Alia admitted, a mix of frustration and sorrow in her voice. "And now, I've been trying to reach his Dubai number, but it's switched off. Where is he? Has he reached the USA?"

Aditya's tone turned sombre as he said, "He texted you from the airport, and you replied, telling him to go to hell."

"I was furious," Alia confessed, grappling with her emotions. "But why? Please, just tell me where he is. I've been calling him nonstop, but his number is unreachable."

Aditya's voice cracked, and tears seemed to mingle with his words, "Maybe he did go to hell…"

Alia's confusion was evident. "What? What do you mean?"

Amidst sobs, Aditya managed to explain, "I don't know if you've seen the news. The plane Sid was on had trouble during the take-off. Despite my desperate attempts to contact him, it was to no avail."

Alia's anxiety escalated. She urgently switched on the TV to catch a breaking news update. Her face contorted in shock and despair as the reality unfolded before her eyes.

BREAKING NEWS:

A tragic plane crash has sent shockwaves around the world. The flight, AI7799 from Dubai to Los Angeles has reportedly crashed, leaving no survivors. The accident occurred a mere five minutes after the take-off, and the authorities are currently investigating the causes behind this heart-wrenching accident. The world mourns the loss of lives cut short in this devastating tragedy.

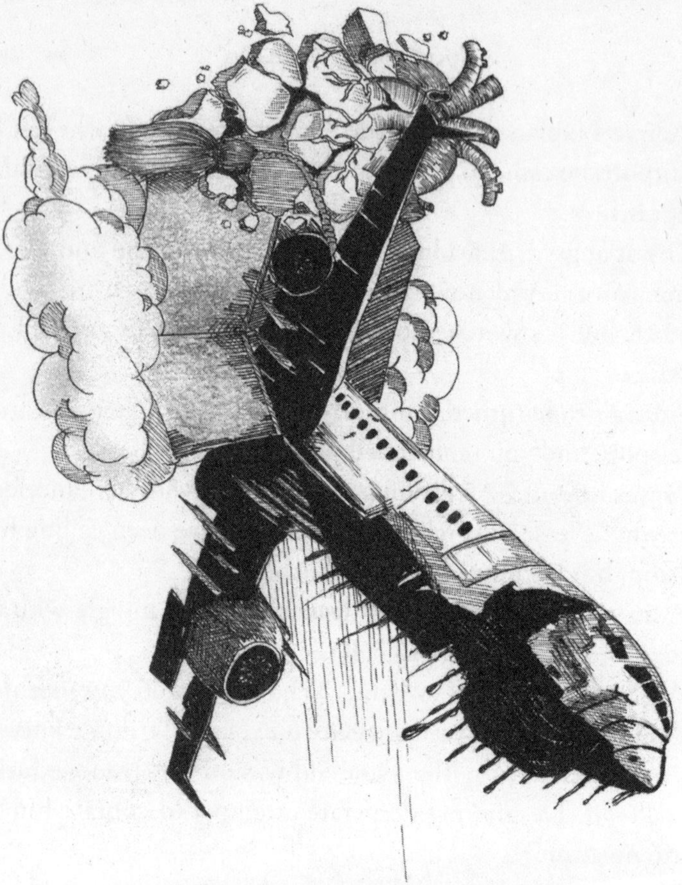

Alia's voice quivered with disbelief. "What? No!" Her words escalated into a scream, a mixture of shock and anguish merging as tears flowed freely.

Aditya's voice was gentle but strained. "I think Siddhartha had an apprehension, and that's why he messaged me from the airport, to give you, his diary. Alia? Alia?"

But Alia's response was just drowned in heavy sobs. The weight of the news had taken its toll, rendering her speechless. Eventually, she managed to choke out a few words. "This can't be happening... this can't be real."

Aditya's desperation grew, but the line remained silent. "Alia? Please, say something."

Her voice, heavy with grief, struggled through the tears. "I... I cannot... I can't believe it." And with that, the connection shattered as she abruptly cut the call, her sorrow too immense to be contained in mere words.

Aditya made numerous attempts to reach out to Alia in the aftermath, but every call went unanswered. Her whereabouts remained a mystery, and he was left wondering about her well-being. His heart felt heavy with the burden of uncertainty, and the thought of facing her was equally daunting. Perhaps it was wiser for them to stay apart for a while.

It is as though Sid and Alia's love story was marked by an unexplainable curse. Despite their profound affection, their paths seemed fated to never intertwine. In a cruel twist of destiny, their love remained unfulfilled. Aditya held onto a hope that in another life, his dear friend will finally find his Alia, unburdened by the obstacles of this world.

Alia stumbled upon one final poem within the diary, a composition that seemed to carry a premonition of his tragic fate. The verses echoed with an eerie poignancy, hinting that maybe, just maybe, Sid had an inkling of what was to come.

I waited because
you asked me to
but there was no tomorrow.

After hanging up the phone, Aditya remembered how he had talked to Siddhartha. It felt like he was alive minutes earlier and now suddenly he was gone, and no one can ever do anything about it.

Sid: Hi Aditya. I am very afraid. I am going on a new journey leaving Alia and my mother behind, all alone. What if I fail?

Aditya: What are you talking about? It will be fine. Do not panic.

Sid: I wanted to talk to Alia, but I do not want to scare her. Also, her last message to me was "go to hell." Maybe I am going there. See, I am sending you the screenshot. She is so angry with me.

Screenshot attached.

Aditya: What are you talking about? Hell?

Sid: I do not have much time. I am in the immigration queue. I must go now.

Aditya: You do have time. Nothing will happen to you. It will be all fine.

Sid: I do not know that, but please give the diary to Alia today…

Aditya: Are you there?

Sid: Typing……..

Connection Ends

Maybe next time,
in another life,
we will meet again,
where hearts will not ache,
and the pain will find an end.
So maybe in another life,
we will find,
the love that we sought,
in this life, left behind.

Alia.

The flashbacks,
the night attacks,
the voice of yours
cannot let me move on,
can I ever change,
or will I remain the same?
I just hope I meet
you soon.

Tears fall
like rain
from my eyes
but the memories of you
will never die
my love,
will never die.

12th April, 2022

Dear diary,

I am Alia. Siddhartha's Alia. The one he loved more than anything in this world. The one he always mentioned to you. The one who knew him inside and out, who shared his dreams, his passions, his fears. The one who was his soulmate, his companion, his everything. The one who never got to read his words until it was too late. Too late, do you understand what that means? He is gone now. Gone forever and snatched away from me by a cruel twist of fate.

My heart is shattered into a million pieces. Siddhartha boarded the doomed plane that crashed on its way to the USA. He was so excited to pursue his studies there, have influence in the world, and fulfil his potential. He had worked so hard for this opportunity and had sacrificed so much. He had so many plans, so many hopes, so many dreams. And they were all destroyed in an instant. All his dreams vanished like smoke.

I have been in the hospital for three days. When I heard the news, I could not believe it at first. I thought it was a mistake, a prank, a nightmare. But it was real. It was the most horrible thing that has ever happened to me. I collapsed on the spot and woke up in a hospital bed. They told me I had a nervous breakdown and that I needed to rest and recover. But how can I rest when my heart is bleeding? How can I recover when my soul is broken?

I cannot describe how much I miss him in this lonely world. I never thought I would have to face a day when the love of my life would be on the other side of the world. A world where I cannot see him, touch him, hear him, feel him—a world where he is no longer alive.

I am planning to go to Jordan forever and be with my family. I cannot live alone in Dubai, where I have memories of us everywhere. This city haunts me. This city is eating me alive. Every street, every corner, every place reminds me of him. Of our laughter, our tears, our moments. Of the first time we met, the first time we kissed, the first time we said, "I love you." Of the last time we hugged, the last time we smiled, the last time we said "goodbye."

I do not even dare to talk to Siddhartha's mom. I cannot even imagine how she must be feeling after losing her only son. The son who was her pride, her joy, her life. The son who had such a bright future ahead of him, who had such a kind heart and a brilliant mind. Her son who loved me like no one else ever did. I can only pray to God to give her immense strength to bear this unbearable loss.

I do not know what to do with myself. I do not know how to live without him. I do not know how to breathe without him.

He was my everything.

And now he is gone.

Gone forever.

Hopelessly,

Alia.

In the randomness of the world,
I lost my heart to you
who could not be mine
just because
loving you was a sin,
in today's time.

13th April, 2022

You were as pure
as you could be
surreal than my dreams
I wish I can hold you
but then I woke up
from a monstrous dream
realising that day can never come
where you can be with me

Dear diary,

I cannot take it anymore. I don't like the constant calls, messages, and reminders of what I have lost. I won't say that I like Aditya's voice, pity, and concern. He thinks he is helping me, but he is only hurting me more.

He was the one who broke the news to me. He was the one who told me that Siddhartha was gone. He was the one who shattered my world. He was Siddhartha's best friend.

But I do not want his sorry. I do not want his wishes. I do not want his concern. I do not want his brotherhood.

I want Siddhartha. I want him back. I want him alive.

But he is not coming back. He is not alive.

He is dead. And so am I.

I blocked Aditya's number that day as he constantly called me. I have deleted all my social media accounts. I have switched off my phone. I have cut off all contact with the outside world.

I do not want to talk to anyone. I do not want to see anyone. I do not want to hear anyone.

I want to be alone.
Alone with my pain.
Alone with my grief.
Alone with my guilt.

I blame myself for Siddhartha's death. I blame myself for letting him go. I blame myself for not being there for him. I should have gone with him to the USA. I should have supported him in his dreams. I should have told him how much I loved him.

He may have still been here.
We may have still been happy.
We could have still been together.
But we are not.
We are apart.
We are broken.
We are nothing.
I have nothing left to live for.
I have no reason to go on.
I have no hope to cling to.
I have no will to survive.
I want to end this misery.

Alia.

You are a moon in my universe,
because now I can only
love you from a distance.

15th April, 2022

Dear diary,

I cannot believe what my father has done. He has found out about Siddhartha's death, and he is not even sorry. He is not even sad. He is not even sympathetic.

He is happy.

Happy that the problem has been solved.

Happy that the obstacle has been removed.

Happy that the disgrace has been erased.

He thinks that Siddhartha was a mistake, a sin, a curse. He thinks that Siddhartha was nothing, nothing at all.

But he is wrong.

Siddhartha was everything, everything to me.

He was my love, my life, my soul.

He was my happiness, my peace, my hope.

He was my reason, my purpose, my meaning.

He was everything.

And now he is gone.

Gone forever.

And my father does not care.

He does not care about my feelings. He does not care about my pain. He does not care about my loss.

He only cares about his reputation. He only cares about his pride. He only cares about his honour.

He wants me to come back to Jordan and marry someone else. He wants me to forget Siddhartha and move on. He wants me to pretend that nothing has happened and start over.

But I cannot do that. I will not do that. I do not want to do that.

I do not want to come back to Jordan and marry someone else. I do not want to forget Siddhartha and move on. I do not want to pretend that nothing happened and start over.

I want to remember Siddhartha and honour him. I want to accept that something has happened and end it properly.

I want to end it all.

I want to end this pressure. I want to end this torture. I want to end this life.

I want to end it now.

My father is calling me every day. He is yelling at me, threatening me, extorting me. He is saying that if I do not come back, he will disown me, he will cut me off, he will curse me.

He is saying that I have no choice, no voice, no rights.

He is saying that I must obey him, respect him, follow him.

But he is wrong.

I have a choice, a voice, a right.

I have the choice to say no, the voice to say stop, the right to say enough.

I have the choice to live my own way, the voice to express my own feelings, the right to pursue my own happiness.

I have the choice to love Siddhartha, the voice to praise Siddhartha, the right to be with Siddhartha.

And I will make that choice soon.

Alia.

18th April, 2022

Dear diary,

I cannot take it anymore. I cannot live without Siddhartha. He was my everything, and now he is gone. Gone forever. Gone without a goodbye.

I miss him so much that it hurts. It hurts more than anything in this world. It hurts more than death itself.

I want to see him so badly that it drives me crazy. It drives me crazy more than anything in this world. It drives me crazy more than madness itself.

But I have no way to see him. No way to talk to him, hear him, or touch him. No way to find him or be with him or love him.

He has gone to heaven. Gone forever. Gone without me.

He has gone to heaven, and I want to go with him.

I want to go with him, and I have decided to do it.

I have decided to end my life and join him in heaven.

I have decided to end my misery and find my happiness.

I have decided to end this nightmare and start a dream.

A dream of Siddhartha.

But before I do it, I want to write to you one last time. I want to tell you how much you mean to me, how much you have helped me, how much you have listened to me.

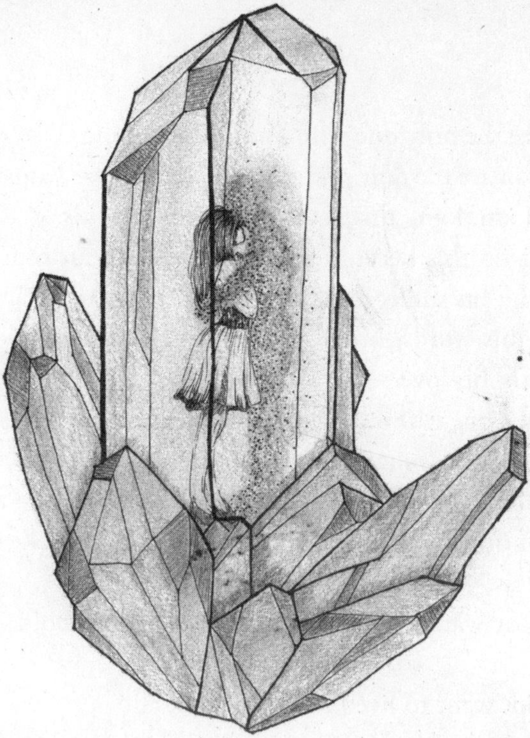

You are my diary, but you are also my friend. You are my friend, but you are also my confidant. You are my confidant, but you are also my therapist.

You are the only one who knows everything about me and Siddhartha. You are the only one who knows how we met, how we fell in love, how we faced the challenges. You are the only one who knows how we fought, how we made up, how we stayed together.

You are the only one who knows how happy we were, how happy we made each other, how happy we could have been.

You are the only one who knows how sad I am, how sad he made me, how sad I will always be.

You are the only one who knows how much I love him, how much he loved me, how much we loved each other.

You are the only one who knows everything.

And you are the only one who will know why I am doing this.

Why I am doing this, and why I must do this.

I must do this because I cannot live without him. I cannot live without his smile, his laugh, his kisses. I cannot live without his voice, his words, his vows. I cannot live without his touch, his warmth, his love.

I cannot live without him.

And I do not want to live without him.

I do not want to live in this world that took him away from me. I do not want to live in this world that is cruel, unfair, and meaningless.

I do not want to live in this world that is cold, dark, and lonely.

I do not want to live in this world at all.

I want to live in heaven with him. I want to live in heaven where he is waiting for me. I want to live in heaven where he is smiling at me, laughing with me, kissing me.

I want to live in heaven where he is talking to me, listening to me, understanding me.

I want to live in heaven where he is touching me, warming me, loving me.

I want to live in heaven with him.

And I will do it soon.

Very soon.

Goodbye Diary.

Goodbye world.

Hello Siddhartha.

I love you.

But as soon as I wrote these words, as soon as I closed the diary, as soon as I reached for the pills, I woke up. I woke up from a deep sleep, from a vivid dream, from a horrible nightmare. It was all a nightmare. A nightmare that felt so real, so intense, so terrifying. But it was not real. It was not true. It was not happening. I was not going to kill myself. I was not going to join Siddhartha in heaven. I was not going to end it all.

I was alive. I was awake. I was here sweating in my room. But I could not forget him. And I could not move on without him. And I could not die either. Because even though I wanted to die and be with him, I knew that it was wrong. Wrong for me and wrong for him.

Wrong for me because it would be selfish, cowardly, and wasteful. Wrong for me because it would hurt my family and friends and everyone who cares about me. Wrong for me because it would deny my chance of living and growing and healing.

Wrong for him because it would dishonour his memory and his sacrifice and his dream. Wrong for him because it would break his heart and his soul and his spirit. Wrong for him because it would betray his love and his trust and his hope.

He loved me too much to want me to die. He loved me too much to want me to suffer. He loved me too much to want me to give up.

He wanted me to live. He wanted me to be happy. He wanted me to hope.

He wanted me to live for him, be happy for him, hope for him.

He wanted me to live for us, be happy for us, hope for us.

He wanted me to live for our love, be happy for our love, hope for our love.

And I wanted that too.

I wanted that more than anything in this world.

I wanted that more than death itself.

And that is why I woke up.

I woke up from the nightmare and into the reality.

A reality that was hard, painful, and lonely, but also a reality that was possible, hopeful, and meaningful.

A reality where I was alive and he was dead, but also a reality where I was still his and he was still mine.

A reality where we were apart but also together, in heart, soul, and spirit.

A reality where we still had a chance, a chance to find each other again, a chance to be together again, a chance to love each other again.

A chance that I would not waste, a chance that I would not lose, a chance that I would not let go.

A chance that I would fight for, a chance that I would live for, a chance for which I would die.

A chance for us.

A chance for our love.

A chance for our dream.

A dream of Siddhartha.

Alia.

20th April, 2022

I am left at the crossroads
thinking about my life
were you even real
or fragment of my mind?
were we even destined to meet
or were we just passing time?

Dear diary,

I do not know what to do. I feel like I am standing at a crossroads, with two paths leading to two different worlds, two different lives, two different choices. I feel like I am trapped in a cage, with no way out, no escape, no solution.

My father is in the hospital. He collapsed on the floor, clutching his chest, gasping for air. He had a heart attack, and he is in a critical condition. He is hooked to machines, tubes, and wires. He is fighting for his life, and he is asking for me.

He called me yesterday, and his voice was weak, shaky, and desperate.

"Alia, my daughter, please come back to Jordan and see me. Please, I beg you. I love you, and I miss you. I am sorry for everything I have ever done to you. I want to make up for everything. Please, give me a chance."

But I do not believe him. I do not trust him. I do not forgive him.

He has hurt me too much. He has betrayed me too often. He has rejected me too harshly.

He has never accepted my love for Siddhartha. He has never respected my choice to be with him. He has never supported my decision to stay in Dubai.

He has always tried to control me, manipulate me, pressurise me. He has always tried to force me to marry someone else, someone I do not love, someone I do not want.

He has always hated Siddhartha, insulted him, cursed him. He has always blamed him for everything, accused him of everything, wished him dead.

And now he is dead.

Siddhartha is dead.

And my father does not care.

He does not care about my feelings. He does not care about my pain. He does not care about my loss.

He only cares about himself. He only cares about his health. He only cares about his will.

He wants me to come back to Jordan and marry someone else. He wants me to forget Siddhartha and move on. He wants me to obey him, respect him, follow him.

But I cannot do that. I will not do that. I do not want to do that.

I want to stay in Dubai and mourn Siddhartha. I want to remember Siddhartha and honour him. I want to accept that something happened and end it.

I want to end it all.

I want to end this pressure. I want to end this torture. I want to end this life.

I want to end it now.

But I cannot do that either. I cannot be so selfish. I cannot be so cruel.

He is still my father. He is still my blood. He is still my family.

He gave me life, he raised me, he educated me.

He loved me, he cared for me, he protected me.

He did everything for me, he sacrificed everything for me, he wanted the best for me.

He did it all in his own way, his own style, his own belief.

He did it all because he thought it was right, it was good, it was best.

He did it all because he loved me.

And I love him too.

I love him despite everything, despite anything, despite nothing.

I love him because he is my father, my blood, my family.

And I cannot let him die alone, without seeing me, without talking to me.

I cannot let him die with regret, with anger, with bitterness.

I cannot let him die without peace, without forgiveness, without love.

I must go back to Jordan and see him. I must talk to him and listen to him. I must forgive him and love him.

I must do it for him.

I must do it for myself.

I must do it for Siddhartha.

Siddhartha would want me to do it. Siddhartha would understand why I must do it. Siddhartha would support me in doing it.

Siddhartha loved me unconditionally, completely, eternally.

Siddhartha wanted me to be happy, peaceful, hopeful.

Siddhartha wished me the best, the good, the right.

Siddhartha was everything for me, everything to me, everything with me.

And he still is.

He still loves me from the heaven, from beyond, from within.

He still wants me from the heaven, from beyond.

Alia.

22nd April 2022

Dear diary,

Today, I had to face my father, who was lying on his deathbed, and listen to his last wish. A wish that broke my heart and shattered my soul.

He asked me to promise him something. Something that I could never do. Something that I would never want to do.

He asked me to promise him I would marry someone else. Someone that he had chosen for me. Someone that I had never met, never seen, never loved.

He asked me to promise him that I would forget Siddhartha. Siddhartha, who was my true love, my soulmate, my everything.

Siddhartha, who was dead.

He said that it was for my good. That it was for my happiness. That it was for my future.

He said that he loved me, and he wanted me to be happy. He said that he was sorry for everything he had done to me. He said he was proud of me and wanted me to succeed.

He said that he knew I loved Siddhartha and respected that. He said he knew that Siddhartha loved me and admired that. He said that he knew that we were happy together, and he envied that.

But he also said that Siddhartha was gone and would never come back. He said that I had to move on and start a new life. He said I had to let go of the past and embrace the present.

He said that he had found a suitable match for me. A man who was wealthy, handsome, educated, and respectful. A man who belonged to our culture, our religion, our community. A man who would care for, protect, and cherish me.

He said that he had arranged everything for me. A wedding date, a wedding venue, a wedding dress. He said he invited all our relatives, friends, and neighbours.

He said he wanted me to promise him that I would marry this man, that I would love this man, that I would forget Siddhartha.

He said that it was his dying wish. That it was his final request. That it was his only hope.

He looked at me with his weak eyes and held my hand with his frail fingers. He begged me with his soft voice and pleaded with his sincere words,

"Please promise me, Alia. Please promise me before I die."

I did not know what to say. I did not know what to do. I did not know how to react. I felt a whirlwind of emotions: anger, sadness, confusion, compassion. I was angry at him for asking me such a thing. How could he expect me to marry someone else when I only loved Siddhartha? How could he expect me to forget Siddhartha when he was the only reason I lived? How could he expect me to betray Siddhartha when he was the only one who understood me?

I was sad for him for being so sick. He looked so frail, so weak, so helpless. He was dying, and he knew it. He was scared, and he showed it. He was lonely, and he felt it.

I was confused by him for being so contradictory. He said he loved me, but he hurt me. He said he respected me, but he controlled me. He said he envied me, but he blamed me.

I was compassionate for him for being so human. He made mistakes, and he regretted them. He had flaws, and he admitted them. He had hopes, and he expressed them.

He was my father, and I loved him.

But I also loved Siddhartha.

And I could not promise him what he wanted.

I could not promise him that I would get married to someone else.

I could not promise him that I would forget Siddhartha.

I could not promise him that I would be happy without Siddhartha.

I looked at him with my tearful eyes and squeezed his hand with my trembling fingers. I spoke with my broken voice and answered with my honest words,

"I am sorry, father. I am sorry, but I cannot promise you that."

He opened his eyes and saw my face. He heard my voice and understood my words. He felt my hand and sensed my pain but did not say a word. He turned his eyes away from me in utter disappointment.

I do not know if my family will ever understand what Siddhartha meant to me. They think I am a juvenile, and if I marry someone, I can forget Siddhartha and move on.

Alia.

Were we soulmates
or maybe twin flames?
Were we just lovers
trying to get intimate?
Were we just friends
who knew deep secrets
or were we just two strangers
who randomly met?

23rd April, 2022

Dear diary,

I have lost all sense of time in this hellhole. I have no idea where my family has taken me or what they want from me. All I know is that I must escape. All I have is you. They have confiscated my phone, my passport, my belongings.

I have been locked in my room with no way to contact the outside world. My captors are my own family and friends, the people who are supposed to love and protect me. But they have betrayed me.

They have told me that they are saving me from a terrible fate and protecting me from the world's dangers. But I know the truth. They are enslaving me. They want to control me, to dictate my life.

They have tried to break me, brainwash me, coerce me. But I have refused to bend. I have held on to my identity, values, and love for Siddhartha.

Siddhartha is the only reason I am still alive. He is the light in the darkness, the hope that sustains me. He is the one who makes me want to fight, to survive, to escape.

I will not give up. I will not let them break me. I will survive this for me, for him, and us. I will not marry anyone.

Alia.

25th April, 2022

Dear diary,

Today, my sister, Hania, came to my room to check on me. She felt guilty as she told our father about Siddhartha a couple of months back, which is how he had learned about us. He had never been supportive of my decision and used to curse him repeatedly.

I did not want to speak to her, but she was crying so inconsolably that I thought to give her a chance to explain why she did that.

Hania told me that when I disclosed my love for Sid over the phone, dad passed by, and he heard bits about what we were discussing. After my call, he interrogated Hania and threatened her to speak the truth. She tried making up some stories but, in the end, gave in as she knew how much our dad hated us lying. Dad created a lot of drama that day in the house. He shouted at everyone, especially at our mother. He claimed that sending me to Dubai was his biggest mistake. He regretted giving me so much freedom. Since that day, he has been on a mission to search for a groom within our community for me.

Mom tried to explain to him, but all in vain. So, my entire family thought it was better to obey our father and do what he said. But suddenly, in the last few months, his health took a toll, and he had to be hospitalised. The doctor gravely told him that he had few days to live and he would be lucky if he survived a month.

So, he was left with no choice but to tell everything to his elder brother, who now has taken an oath to get me married to the selected groom within the few days that my father is alive. On knowing this, I could not fight back my tears.

What will I do now? Why did I agree to come to Jordan? I should have thought about my family's old values and traditions. They would not change. They can never change.

I am feeling so scared. Diary, what will I do if I have to marry the man that my family has selected? How will I accept this? How can I let anyone other than Siddhartha touch me? I do not know how to escape from this place.

Why did I ever come here? I am so scared and lonely. I wish he would give me some sign from beyond and help me come out of this. I wish I were dead.

Alia.

They say time will make it better,
but
will it ever?

27th April, 2022

Dear diary,

Today, I was allowed to go to the living room to have food instead of them slipping it into my room. My uncle thought that I was no longer a threat and should be allowed to roam around in the house. All the landline phones have been disconnected. I cannot use a mobile phone, laptop, or computer.

My mother, Hania, and I were having lunch when my mother asked me about Siddhartha, as we had never spoken about him. All she got to know about him was from my father, and she never enquired on her own. But she felt unfortunate seeing me in this condition. So, she started a conversation related to that fateful day. She wanted to know if I took him to the airport, what were his last words, how did I get to know about his demise, etc.

But while telling her the ordeal, something struck me. I felt the same restlessness that I had felt when Siddhartha was alive. I do not know how to explain this feeling, but it felt extraordinary, as if he was still breathing in the same world where I was breathing. But how can that be true?

I brushed off the thoughts and continued with my day. I hope to meet Sid on the other side soon.

Alia.

If we ever meet each other again,
I promise I will not let you go.

Siddhartha

While I embarked on a new journey,
I was met with the wildest twists, turns,
and so many what ifs
I do not know where to go from here
I have come too far
So, I will take my next step
into the world that seems thousand miles apart.

09th April, 2022

Dear new diary,

I am writing to you from the airport. I missed my flight. Why? You might ask. It was a nightmare that I never want to relive again.

It all started when I was supposed to board the flight that would take me to the USA. I was so excited and nervous but also confident and ready. I had packed everything I needed, said goodbye to everyone I loved, and prepared myself for the journey of a lifetime.

I was waiting in line for my immigration check, holding my passport and all other documents I would need. I had checked them a hundred times before, ensuring everything was in order. I had no reason to worry, or so I thought.

When it was my turn, I handed over my documents to the officer with a smile. He scanned them and looked at me with a frown. He said that, among the papers, I-20, a document certifying that a student has been admitted to a full-time study programme in the United States, was missing. And it was an essential document for student travellers to be included.

I felt a surge of panic and confusion. I looked at the documents and realised that he was right. How could I have missed that? In all the chaos and emotions, I forgot to take a printout.

The officer told me I needed a signed I-20 to board the flight. He said it was a violation, and I had to be taken to a detention centre for further investigation. He said that they had to contact my college to verify my admission status. He said it could take hours before they could clear me due to the time difference between the USA and Dubai.

I tried to explain, to apologise, to plead. But it was of no use. He removed me from the immigration queue and escorted me to a separate room. The security personnel at the entrance took away my cell phone and luggage for security reasons and escorted me inside. He said he would be back soon but did not say when.

I was alone, scared, and helpless. I could not contact anyone to tell them where I was or what had happened. I did not know what would happen to me or how long it would take. I had no way of escaping or fixing this mess.

I spent a couple of hours at the airport, feeling like a prisoner, a criminal, a fool. The only people who talked to me were the immigration officers who contacted my college for the official discussion. They asked me all kinds of questions; some were suspicious, and some were polite and sympathetic. They told me they were trying to resolve the issue as soon as possible but warned me that it could take longer than expected.

They only allowed me to leave the detention centre once the matter was resolved. They only allowed me to use my phone or access my luggage once they cleared me. They did not allow me to have any contact with the outside world until they released me.

Finally, after what seemed like an eternity, they told me they had verified my admission status with my college and received a signed copy of my I-20 by email. They told me they had cleared me for travel and booked me on the next available flight to the

USA. They told me they were sorry for the inconvenience and hoped I would enjoy my stay in the USA. They returned my phone and luggage and escorted me to the boarding gate. They wished me good luck and goodbye.

Your new friend,
Siddhartha.

The world around me
is collapsing
into flames,
into a zone
for which I do not have a name.
Still my breath yearns for you
still my hands
want to touch nothing but you.
I do not how to put out in words
that even in a situation
like this,
my heart is melting for you.

10th April, 2022

Dear new diary,

I am finally sitting at the boarding gate for my flight. The last twelve hours have been eventful. I am feeling very anxious, scared, and sad about what I am going to tell you. There is a stir at the airport, and I do not know what to do.

I have just learned the most shocking and terrifying news of my life. The flight I was supposed to take yesterday to the USA has crashed. There were no survivors. Everyone onboard was killed.

I cannot believe it. I cannot accept it. I cannot imagine it.

How could this happen? How could this happen to me? How could this happen to them?

They were innocent people with hopes and dreams, families and friends, lives and loves.

They did not deserve this fate. They did not deserve this horror.

They could have been me. I could have been them.

I was so close to being on that flight. I was so close to being dead.

But I was not. I was not on that flight. I was not dead.

I am alive.

But I do not feel alive. I feel numb, empty, hollow.

I feel guilty, angry, sad.

I feel like I have cheated death but also cheated life.

I feel like I have escaped a nightmare but have also entered a nightmare.

I cannot even imagine thinking about my mother and Alia. How would they have reacted when they assumed I was on that dreadful flight? They would have cried their eyes out and screamed and mourned.

They would have thought that I was dead and perished in the crash. They would have thought that they had lost me forever. They must have been devastated, heartbroken, shattered. They must have prayed, hoped, wished.

I switched on my phone and saw endless messages from my mother and Aditya. I called Aditya, as he would have told Alia as well. I called him ten times, and, in the end, I could finally connect to him. He told me that he delivered the diary to Alia and even broke out the news of my death, and since that last call, Alia's phone has been switched off. I also tried to call Alia, but it was switched off.

Yours,
Siddhartha.

I do not know
how to feel,
whether to smile
or to grieve.
Even though
I have not lost a thing
but deep in my heart
I feel I have lost a piece.

10th April, 2022

Dear new diary,

I had to stop writing when I was asked to board the flight. Finally, I am flying towards my dream: the USA. I managed to connect with my mother. It was the most emotional and heartbreaking conversation I have ever had. She was shocked, relieved, and happy to hear my voice. She told me about her nightmare when she learned that the flight I was supposed to be on, had crashed.

She said she saw the news on TV and immediately recognised the flight number and the airline. She felt a cold shiver run down her spine and dropped the remote control. She tried calling me repeatedly, but my phone was unreachable. She panicked, screamed, and prayed for my life.

She also tried contacting Alia, but her phone was switched off. She spoke to Aditya, and they both cried incessantly over the phone. Aditya offered to come to India to be with her for a few days, so that she could cope with my death.

She felt like her whole world had ended and she had nothing left to live for. She had wished to die too and join me in heaven. She had cursed God, fate, and life.

She spent the next few hours in a state of shock and grief. She did not eat or talked to anyone. She had only cried, mourned, and suffered.

When I called her, she thought it was a prank or a hallucination. She did not believe it was me until I told her the situation, and only then was she convinced. She was overjoyed and grateful and blessed. She hugged the phone and thanked God, fate, and life.

She asked me the entire story of what happened. She listened to my story with awe and disbelief. She was amazed by my luck, courage, and determination.

She told me how much she loved, missed, and wanted me more than anything in this world. She told me how proud she was of me for pursuing my dream, overcoming my challenges, and achieving my goals.

She asked me about Alia and if I had contacted her till now. Knowing that I had not yet contacted her, she asked me to immediately call her and relieve her of the pain that she might be suffering due to the tragic news of the flight crash.

She wanted me to be happy, to enjoy my stay in the USA, and to make the most of my opportunity.

She wanted us to stay in touch, talk often, and share our feelings.

She also wanted us to reunite again as a family, a team, and an unit.

She said all these things with so much love and emotion in her voice that I could not help but cry, too.

I cried tears of joy, relief, sorrow, and regret.

I cried because I was happy to hear from her but sad to leave her alone.

I cried because I was relieved to be alive but also guilty for being alive.

I cried because I felt everything at once but also nothing at all.

I cried because I was alive.

Yours,
Siddhartha.

I know it has been days,
but I feel it has been months;
when I think hard
it feels maybe years
since we cried out tears
because loving you was a sin
and I have no clue
on how to keep you alive
in my thoughts
from deep within.

11th April, 2022

Dear new diary,

I have reached the USA and tried everything to contact Alia, but I need help to get through. She is unreachable, untraceable, and invisible. She has disappeared from my life, and I do not know if she will ever return.

I called her from the airport several times. I was so excited and nervous to call her, hear her voice, and tell her the truth. I hoped that she would answer, she would listen, and she would forgive.

Her phone was switched off. Every time I called her, I got the same message: "The number you have dialled is unavailable. Please try again later." I tried repeatedly, but it was always the same. No answer. No response. No connection.

I wondered if she had changed her number. She does not know that I am alive. Aditya had told her about my death, and after that, Alia's phone had been switched off.

Aditya tried contacting her via the hotel where we stayed. The hotel representative said that after Aditya met her at her hotel, she instructed them not to let anyone know about her whereabouts and that she did not want to meet any visitors.

I decided to try other ways to contact her. I searched for her on social media but could not find her. She has either deleted all her accounts or has blocked me off all. She has cut off all ties with me, or at least hidden all traces of me. I wonder why she had done that or when she did that.

I feel so frustrated and desperate. I feel like there was no way to contact her, no way to reach out to her, no way to find her. I feel like I have lost her forever, and I do not know what to do.

I love her so much, and I miss her so much. I want her so much, and I need her so much.

She is my everything, and without her, I am nothing. She is my reason to live, and without her, I have no reason. She is my hope to survive, and without her, I have no hope. She is my dream to be happy, and without her, I have no dream. She is my Alia, and without her, I am not me. But she does not know that. She does not feel that. She does not want that. She does not know that I am alive, that I love her, and that I want her more than anything in this world.

It breaks my heart into a million pieces. And it hurts so much. It hurts more than anything in this world. It hurts more than death itself. And I do not know how to stop it. I do not know how to heal it. I do not know how to live with it. I do not know how to live at all.

Yours,
Siddhartha.

No matter where I go,
my heart searches for you;
my eyes try to find you within the crowd
and whatever I try to do,
my silly heart takes me back to the day
when I left you
on that starry dark night.

12th April, 2022

Dear new diary,

I am alone in this nightmare, with no hope, no peace, no escape. I am alone, and I hate it. I hate being alone in this cold and dark place where no one knows me, cares for me, or loves me. I hate being alive in this cruel and unfair world, where nothing goes my way, nothing makes sense, nothing matters. I hate being here in this foreign and hostile land, where everything is strange, challenging, and different.

I want to go back. I want to return to Dubai, where everything is familiar, comfortable, and in my routine. Where I have a home, a family, a life. Where I have friends, hobbies, and dreams. And where I have Alia.

I want to return to my mother, where everything was warm, loving, and safe. Where she hugged me, kissed me, praised me. Where she cooked for me, cared for me, and supported me, where she loved me.

I want to return to Alia, where everything is beautiful, happy, and perfect. Where she smiled at me, laughed with me, kissed me. Where she talked to me, listened to me, and understood me. Where she loved me.

But I cannot go back. I cannot go back to the past that is gone forever. I cannot go back to the people who are lost forever. I cannot go back to the love that is broken forever.

I can only go forward. Forward into the unknown, the uncertain, the unpredictable. Forward to the USA, where everything is new, different, and strange. Where I have no home, no family, no life. Where I have no friends, no hobbies, no dreams. Where I have no Alia.

Forward to college, where everything is challenging, demanding, and stressful. Where I must study hard, work hard, and compete hard. Where I must prove myself, improve myself, and survive. Where I must be someone else.

Forward into my future, where everything is unclear, doubtful, and scary. I am still determining what will happen, what will change, or what will end. And I am still determining what I want, what I need, and what I hope. I need to find out who I am.

In my life, everything is hard, painful, and lonely. I must face the reality, the consequences, and the truth. I must deal with the loss, with the guilt, with the regret. Where I must live without Alia.

Forward into nothing at all. Into nothing that matters. Nothing that makes sense. Nothing that makes me happy.

But I have no choice. I have no choice but to go forward. I have no choice but to live on. I have no choice but to survive.

Because maybe there is still a chance for me.

It was a chance for me to find a way to contact Alia and tell her that I am alive, that I love her, and that I want her more than anything in this world.

A chance for me to find a way out of this nightmare and into a dream.

A dream of Alia.

But until then, I am alone in this nightmare, with no hope, peace, or escape. I am alone.

And I hate it.

Yours,
Siddhartha.

Do you miss me
like I miss you?
Do you yearn for me
like I do?
why love did this to us
when it
was not meant to?

14th April, 2022

Dear new diary,

I cannot stop thinking about Alia. I wonder what she is going through, how she feels, and what she is doing. I wonder if she is safe, happy, or even alive.

I have nightmares every night. I see her face, her eyes, her smile. I hear her voice, her laugh, her cry. I feel her touch, her warmth, her love.

But then I see her in pain, in fear, in despair. I hear her scream, sob, curse. I feel her push, hit, reject.

I see her with someone else, someone I do not know, someone she does not love. I hear her say his name, his words, his vows. I feel her kiss him, hug him, marry him.

I see her die alone, without me. I hear her last breath, last word, previous wish. I feel her soul leave, fade, vanish.

And then I wake up, sweating, shaking, crying. I realise that it was all a dream, a nightmare, a torture.

But then I realised it could also be a reality, a possibility, fate.

And that scares me more than anything.

I miss her so much that it hurts. It hurts like I have never hurt before. It hurts more than death itself.

I want to talk to her so badly that it drives me crazy. It drives me crazy more than anything in this world. It drives me crazy more than madness itself.

But I have no way to reach out to her. No way to call her, text her, or email her. There is no way to find, see, or be with her.

She has gone from my life and gone forever and gone without a trace.

She has gone from my world forever and without a reason.

She has gone from my heart and gone forever and gone without a goodbye.

And I do not know how to bring her back.

I do not know how to live without her.

I do not know how to live at all.

I cannot focus on anything else. Nothing else matters to me. Nothing else makes sense to me.

My classes will start next week, and I need more energy and enthusiasm. But I do not care about my studies, career, or future.

I do not care about myself or anyone else or anything else.

I only care about Alia, but she does not even know that I am alive. I do not know anyone who can help me reach out to her, and it breaks my heart into a million pieces. And it hurts so much.

I do not know how to stop it. I do not know how to heal it. I do not know how to live with it. I do not know how to live at all.

Yours,
Siddhartha.

I wonder when the stars shine
under the moonlit skies
would you still whisper my name
under your breath
so, I can feel you across the breeze
that falls on my face.

15th April, 2022

Dear new diary,

I find it funny how life takes unexpected turns. Just last month, I was in Dubai, juggling my job, GMAT, my interview prep, and my future. And now, I find myself in Los Angeles. This unfamiliar environment has been overwhelmingly chaotic, and on top of that, Alia has gone missing, and I can think of no way to reach out to her. I was walking across the campus yesterday, and I bumped into Alexandria.

Alexandria had helped me a lot in my interview preparation and was the guiding factor in deciding to go with USC for my MBA. I was at the campus library, and she had come in to pick up books. I accidentally bumped into her, causing her to drop her books all over the floor. I apologised and helped her to pick them up. She was so excited to see me but also disappointed because I did not tell her that I had arrived in Los Angeles.

I wanted to tell her what I was going through and why I did not even have time to inform her about my arrival. Still, I decided to give up the explanation as I was already overwhelmed with my life and did not feel ready to share.

I was surprised that we had a good talk, and the more Alexandria and I spoke, the more I realised how much we had in common. She is beautiful, intelligent, and funny. Also, she has a certain charm that makes me feel comfortable around her. I might have

lost the ability to sustain a conversation, but yesterday, I could do so with her. We planned to meet for lunch the next day. Once Alexandria left, I was drawn into the reality. Suddenly, Alia's face came before my eyes, and I could not stop the tears.

Why did I lose her? We were so close to being a forever. Now, I do not even know her trace. What do I do? How do I reach out to her? Shall I fly back to Dubai, stand next to her hotel, and wait until she comes down and show her that I am alive? But I do not even know if she is still living there or has returned to Jordan. I do not have any contact numbers of Alia's friends or family.

I am standing at the crossroads, diary. Please show me the way.

Yours,
Siddhartha.

Even though
I have not seen you
in a while,
every eye I see
reminds me of you,
every face I come across
takes me back to you,
every voice I hear
makes me wonder
if you are just round the corner,
and we will make it through.

25th April, 2022

Dear new diary,

I am writing to you a week after I started college at USC. It was a fresh start, which I very much needed. USC has allowed me to mend my broken heart and work towards my career goals. I was apprehensive about starting at a new school, but joining USC Marshall was the best decision I could ever make for myself. Apart from my studies, Los Angeles is an incredible city, one of some of the most breathtaking places I have ever seen.

Alexandria showed me around the city. She's fantastic, and she knows her way around perfectly. We have visited all the famous landmarks, from the Walk of Fame to the Getty Museum to the Beverly Hills sign. We drove to Griffith Park yesterday and hiked up to the Hollywood Sign. We sat down on a bench and watched the city lights twinkle below. It was a beautiful moment, but I could only think about Alia.

I know I am leading Alexandria on, but I cannot help myself. I am still in love with Alia and do not know how to move on. Alexandria does not know about my past relationship. I need clarifications on it myself. I do not know what to do.

Tonight, I cannot sleep. My mind is racing.

I keep thinking about Alia. I remember her smile, her laugh, her touch. I miss her so much. Where has she gone? Is she safe? Does she miss me like I miss her? Has she moved on?

So many thoughts keep me awake during the night. All these flashbacks keep coming into my mind. Where is Alia?

But I also think about Alexandria. Her hazelnut eyes always attract me towards her. Her brown bun, which she says looks perfect on her, makes me wonder how she would look in open hair. She is active and always wants to go out. She is not at all like Alia. My Alia could spend hours sitting with me in a car. However, Alexandria is always on the move.

Alexandria is a kind and caring person. She deserves to be with someone who loves her unconditionally. I need help to think about both Alia and Alexandria.

But what if I make the wrong choice? What if I hurt the person I love most?

I am so scared.

Yours,
Siddhartha.

My mind is racing,
and my heart is jumping
to come out from within.
Do you still wonder
what we could have been?
Or have you just moved on
sweeping away
all our memories
as if we were nothing.

01st May, 2022

Dear new diary,

It has been a while since I started my journey at USC Marshall, and I must admit, it has been an eventful one. The first few days of school were overwhelming to say the least: lectures, assignments, and deadlines come at you fast. But I am doing my best to keep up with the pace. My cohort here has some of the brightest minds I have ever encountered.

They are focused, hardworking, and driven to achieve excellence. However, sometimes, the competition becomes cutthroat, and everyone is determined in winning at all costs. The idea of making a name for myself and being successful in this new country pushes me to try and give my best, but I am unwilling to cross any lines.

My first lecture on Microeconomics was quite engaging. Our professor, Dr. Kim, is an expert at his craft. He made the subject seem like one of the most fascinating things in the world. Dr. Kim explained the concepts of supply and demand, market equilibrium, and factors of production. He even applied those concepts to everyday situations, making them relatable. On the first day, we had a simple exercise of buying goods with a limited budget, and I realised that every single decision we make can impact the economy. He showed us the importance of price, quality, and availability. It was such a surreal experience. I was engrossed in the class and never wanted it to end. His teaching style helped me understand complex economic concepts. I feel that Dr. Kim is an one-of-a-kind professor.

I have also made some new friends, which has helped me adjust to life in the USA. We attend lectures, study, have coffee breaks, and hang out outside campus. Getting to know these people has enlightened me, and I am happy that they are here with me on this journey. I also found a new house, which has been great. The house is close to campus, spacious, and has fantastic amenities.

My roommates are also from USC, and we have built camaraderie over the past few days. As much as I am enjoying this new chapter of my life, sometimes my thoughts cannot help but drift towards Alia, especially when I remember some of our unforgettable moments. Like one of the last times we spent time together in Dubai, when we went glamping in the dunes. We enjoyed riding camels, exploring the desert, and taking in the breathtaking view of the sunset. Alia made everything seem magical, and we laughed like children while recounting old tales.

Those moments feel like a lifetime ago, and I miss her terribly. I am keeping a positive mindset and taking advantage of everything my new home can offer me. I can only hope that the future holds remarkable things for me, USC, and the beautiful city of Los Angeles.

Till next time,

Siddhartha.

3rd May, 2022

Dear new diary,

Ever since Alia has gone missing, life has been hopeless and meaningless. It has been weeks, and I still miss her immensely. I have tried to contact her but to no avail. It is like she has vanished into thin air, and I do not even know if she is all right.

The placement season is in full swing, and my mind is in turmoil. I cannot focus, and I can barely study. All I think about is Alia and what could have been if we were still together. Desperate for some advice, I reached out to Alexandria. She suggested becoming my case partner and helping me prepare for the placements. I was initially sceptical, given my emotions for Alia, but I also knew I needed all the help I could get.

Our days are now filled with ten hours of college lectures, four hours of case practice, and the remaining time for chores. It is a gruelling routine, but I am determined to give it my all. Alexandria has been helping me understand the cases and genuinely wants me to succeed. It is nice to have someone in my corner, cheering me on, but deep down in my heart, I still want it all to be with Alia.

As the days go by, I am starting to realise how pervasive the pain of heartbreak can be. It echoes through your thoughts, blurs your vision, clouds your judgment, and dulls your desire. Trying to move on from Alia while simultaneously pouring all my energy into case preparation is physically and mentally challenging. The placement season is approaching, and everything is on the line. It is a bleak time and the stakes are high, but I am trying my best to stay positive. I hope for a brighter future, both in terms of professional success and personal happiness.

Yours,
Siddhartha.

4th May, 2022

Dear new diary,

I have been stuck in a rut for months now, and I do not know what to do about it. The pain of losing Alia has been persistent, and I can barely concentrate on anything else, especially the upcoming placement season. I have been busy with case preparation, but it never seems enough to distract me from her thoughts.

The more I try to distract myself, my mind wanders back to her. It is like she is a constant presence in my head. I needed someone to talk to and offer me some advice. So, I called my mother. Even though I tried to avoid the topic of Alia, she could sense my distress. After hearing me out, she advised me to focus on myself and rediscover my goals in life. She reminded me why I wanted to pursue a career in this field and motivated me to keep working.

She also suggested me to try and develop new hobbies or rekindle old ones, anything that can keep me distracted from the pain of heartbreak. She told me that time would heal the wounds and that I needed to keep moving forward. She said that sometimes, the best way to forget someone is by focusing on one's future and working hard towards it. I realised that my mother was right. I have been neglecting my dreams, my aspirations, and my future. Instead of letting the heartbreak consume me, I must find the strength to move on. It is time to put all my energy into the placement season and to work towards achieving my goals.

I know it will not be easy, but I will try. I am grateful for my mother's advice and for having her to rely on, always. I am filled with renewed motivation and the strength to carry on.

Yours,
Siddhartha.

7th May, 2022

Dear new diary,

I cannot believe that it is almost the end of the month. Time is flying by, and I have been running around nonstop. But despite the hectic schedule, I have found time to invest in myself. Alexandria and I have joined the boxing classes at Rumble Los Angeles and rowing classes at Orange Theory. It has been a lot of fun and an excellent way to stay active.

I just found out how much I could enjoy hitting bags. We have also been hitting the gym together, and it feels good to have a workout friend. Alexandria has pushed me to become stronger, and I appreciate the support. What started as a fitness routine has become a bonding experience between us. I am getting to know Alexandria on a deeper level as we share our frustrations, our aspirations, and our stories while we work out. But our routine is going to change next week.

We have to travel to San Francisco for a tech conference. It will be a great learning experience, but I will miss my routine of boxing and gym. I am excited to explore San Francisco. But I will admit that I am nervous too. However, we will likely find some time to stay active and keep our routine intact, even in a new city.

I look forward to discovering unfamiliar places and challenging myself to try new things.

Overall, I am grateful for the friendships and opportunities in my life. I am finding new ways to keep busy, stay motivated, and focus on my goals.

Yours,
Siddhartha.

10th May, 2022

Dear new diary,

I am writing this after returning from the most fun yet emotionally overwhelming trip to San Francisco. Alexandria and I attended a tech conference, which was a great learning experience.

We met many professionals, networked with like-minded people, and attended insightful sessions. After the conference, we decided to explore San Francisco. We walked around Fisherman's Wharf, visited the Golden Gate Bridge, and roamed the Castro District. It was a fantastic experience, and I had a lot of fun until I started seeing Alia all around me.

It was not like she was physically present there, but the city reminded me so much of her. Every couple I saw walking hand in hand, every person with curly hair or similar clothes, and every sigh I heard reminded me of Alia. I shook myself to try to escape it, but it was more complicated than expected. I tried to enjoy the beautiful city, but it wasn't easy with the constant reminders of her.

Thankfully, Alexandria was with me, and she noticed my unease. She was incredibly supportive and helped me stay positive and focused on the beautiful memories that we were making together. She encouraged me to let go of the pain and embrace the beauty of this moment. As the days passed, I slowly started feeling better. I remembered that life was too short to remain stuck in the past, and I committed to focus on the present. On the flight back, I thought about the moments I shared with Alexandria in San Francisco.

I realised that I have a novel support system, new reasons to smile, and new memories to cherish. This trip reminded me that healing takes time, but that does not mean I cannot make the most out of my present.

Yours,
Siddhartha.

15th May, 2022

Dear new diary,

Today, I nervously stepped off the train and looked around, trying to spot Alexandria. I scanned the crowds, searching for her. There was something about her voice that was bright and bubbly.

As we started walking, Alexandria chatted away about all the different buildings and landmarks on campus, telling me all about the history and the architecture. I could tell that she was enthusiastic about the university, and it was contagious.

As we made our way through the campus, I could not help but notice that Alexandria constantly did little things that made me feel special. She would touch my arm when she was excitedly telling me something, or she would laugh at one of my jokes and make eye contact for a little longer than usual. I tried to tell myself that she was just naturally friendly, but something about the way she acted, made me think that maybe she was interested in me.

As we were walking through the beautiful campus gardens, Alexandria suddenly stopped and turned to me. "Can I ask you something?" she said, her cheeks a little pink. "Of course," I said, feeling both excited and nervous.

"Um, well, I was just wondering if you might want to go out sometime? Like, on a date?" she said, looking up at me hopefully. My heart was suddenly racing in my chest. She had just confirmed what I had suspected.

Alexandria looked at me expectantly, waiting for me to answer her question.

"I appreciate the offer, Alexandria. You are a great person to spend time with, but I am not looking to date right now," I replied, trying to be as polite as possible.

"I understand," she said, looking a little bit disappointed. "But if you ever change your mind, you know where to find me."

We continued walking through the campus, but the atmosphere between us had changed a little bit. I could tell that Alexandria was upset by my answer, and I felt guilty for not reciprocating those feelings.

That guilt was compounded by the fact that I was already in love with someone else—Alia.

I did not want to hurt Alexandria's feelings by telling her I was already in love with someone else, but I knew I could not continue leading her on.

As we said goodbye at the end of our tour, I took a deep breath and decided to be honest. "Listen, Alexandria. I want you to know that it is not about you, it is about me. I like someone else, and I do not think it would be fair to either of us to start anything while I still have those feelings," I said, choosing my words carefully.

She nodded, looking understanding. "I appreciate your honesty, and I wish you all the best with your feelings," she said, giving me a reserved smile. As I watched her walk away, I felt relieved that I had finally come clean. It was a difficult conversation, but I knew it was the right thing to do. And, who knows maybe someday, once my feelings for Alia have been resolved, Alexandria and I could revisit the idea of going on a date.

Yours,
Siddhartha.

I know that you are gone,
and there are billions of people
around me
but no one is close enough
to even replace you in my dreams.

18th May, 2022

Dear new diary,

I have sensed that Alexandria has been ignoring me for a week now. I texted her for case practice, and she told me that she was unavailable. She often gives me odd reasons to avoid hanging out.

I should maybe tell her the truth about Alia, as Alexandria thinks I am not dating her on purpose. But how much shall I tell her? Will she believe that Alia has gone missing, and I am still here waiting for her like an old-school, classical hero?

Whenever I feel my life is going to be exemplary, something unexpected happens. After such turmoil, I had finally made a friend, but now she does not want to talk to me. I am always jumping from one maze into the other.

My heart is still with Alia, and till the time it is with her, how can I love someone else? But now, I have to confess the truth about my relationship with Alia and let Alexandria decide if she wants to believe it or not.

Yours,
Siddhartha.

20th May, 2022

Dear new diary,

Today, I finally mustered the courage and confessed about Alia to Alexandria. Alexandria could not believe what had happened to me over the past few months and listened sympathetically. She even searched for Alia on social media, but we could not find her. I told Alexandria that there was no way I could ever find her.

Many of my friends have suggested that I should go on a date with Alexandria. She has been such a great friend, and I enjoy her company. I know she is interested in taking our relationship to the next level, but I am unsure if I am ready. Part of me wants to try it.

I know Alexandria would treat me well and would not hurt me. But my heart is still mourning the loss of Alia. Even though I know deep down that it is over between us, I cannot help but hope that she will return. I know it is not healthy to hold onto the past, and it is unfair to Alexandria. She deserves someone who can give their all to her, and I am not sure if I am ready to do that. I need more time to grieve and heal my broken heart. I also need to focus on myself and my goals.

I have to let go of the past and embrace the present. I fear the future, but I know I need to take one step at a time. I will be ready

to go on that coffee date with Alexandria someday. But for now, I need to focus on healing and moving on.

While I write you about my raw emotions, it has stuck with me that maybe I have lost Alia forever. It is time my heart accepts the truth and moves on. I cannot stand at the same point forever. But what if Alia is still waiting for me? I know it is a hopeless dream, but what is life without dreams?

Yours,
Siddhartha.

26th May, 2022

Dear new diary,

Words cannot express the joy that fills my heart as I write today. My beloved Alia is back in my life, and I can hardly believe this is not some fantastical dream! I had to pinch myself repeatedly to make sure this was not some cruel trick of the mind. When I saw her, I felt a surge of overwhelming emotions—a whirlwind of happiness, relief, and disbelief. We hugged without a second thought, oblivious to the world around us. Tears streamed down our faces as we embraced, each sob a testament to the love that had endured the test of time and distance.

Alia's sudden appearance sent shockwaves through Alexandria, who silently watched our reunion from a distance. I know she must have been grappling with many emotions, but did not want to intrude on this precious moment we were in. We laughed like children, our hearts overflowing with glee as if we had just received the most coveted gifts in the world.

I was consumed by an insatiable curiosity, eager to unravel the mystery of Alia's disappearance. How did she learn of my survival? Her phone was out of reach, and she had vanished from all the social media platforms. My trusted friend, Aditya, had not been in contact with her either. So, how did she find out?

Expectantly, I listened as Alia recounted her harrowing tale, her words painting a vivid picture of her courage and unwavering determination. She revealed the ordeal of being held captive in her own home, her every move monitored, her freedom stolen.

But amidst the darkness, a glimmer of hope emerged. In the chaos following her father's untimely demise, she managed to seize her phone back. She then reactivated her old number, clinging to the possibility that a friend could help her escape the clutches of her oppressive family.

As her phone flickered to life, she was inundated with missed calls and messages from an unfamiliar number. At first, suspicion clouded her mind, fearing someone was playing a cruel prank. Yet, as she delved deeper, she discovered my mother's heartfelt messages, confirming the unbelievable—I was alive. A torrent of emotions swept over her, including guilt, regret, and a burning desire to know why she had unquestioningly accepted Aditya's words and the false news of my demise.

Her mind raced, grappling with unanswered questions, each one fuelling the fire of her determination to escape Jordan. She knew remaining in the country would only increase her family's vigilance, making her escape even more perilous. Yet, she also recognised the grave risks involved in her daring plan. If she failed, the consequences were unimaginable.

Torn between her love for me and the fear of jeopardising her freedom, Alia wrestled with her conscience. Could she confide in her sister or mother? Could she trust them with the truth at all? The weight of these decisions pressed heavily upon her, her mind a battleground of conflicting emotions.

As night fell, she lay awake, her mind being a whirlwind of thoughts, feelings, and scenarios. Sleep eluded her, as her heart pounded in anticipation of the dawn when she would set her plan in motion.

Yours,
Siddhartha.

I do not know whom to trust,
I do not know where to go,
if there is someone in the universe,
help me
find my love,
and this time
I will not let him go

(Alia)

28th May, 2022

Dear new diary,

As dawn approached, the anticipation in Alia's heart grew with each passing moment. The sun, preparing to burst forth with all its brilliance, symbolised the hope within her. Sleep evaded her, as she lay wide awake, determined to escape the clutches of her oppressive circumstances.

Despite her sleepless night, she felt an inexplicable energy coursing through her veins, fuelled by the unwavering belief that she would find her way to me. Even though the path ahead was uncertain, she placed her faith in the universe, trusting that it would guide her toward our reunion.

Alia sought solace in her mother and sister with a newfound resolve, knowing their support was crucial for her daring escapade. Given their deeply-rooted traditional values, she recognised that convincing them to accept her decision would be a formidable challenge. Yet, she remained hopeful that her genuine love for me would eventually touch their hearts.

As Alia poured out her heart, sharing her love for me and the news of me being alive, her mother and sister were deeply moved. They witnessed her conviction and unwavering strength of the flame of love that burned within her. Despite their initial resistance, they began to see the purity of her intentions, realising that her happiness was paramount.

Alia's mother, the family's anchor, was faced with a heart-wrenching decision. She knew that if Alia succeeded in her escape, it would likely mean a lifetime of separation. The thought of never seeing her daughter again sent waves of sorrow through her. However, she also recognised the depth of Alia's love and the unwavering determination in her eyes. With a heavy heart, Alia's mother agreed to support her daughter's daring plan. She knew that while their separation would be painful, it was a sacrifice she was ultimately willing to make for her daughter's happiness.

Together, they embarked on the fragile task of crafting an escape plan, ensuring that every step was calculated to avoid raising suspicion from her watchful uncle.

Alia feigned enthusiasm for the arranged marriage to appease her uncle's concerns, diligently attending wedding preparations and concealing her true intentions. She understood that her uncle's trust was essential for her success, and she played her role with commitment.

One evening, Alia seized an opportunity to propose a trip to Dubai, under the pretence of settling her outstanding affairs from her previous life there. She highlighted the potential legal complications if she remained absent from the company she worked for and the need to remove her belongings from the hotel.

Alia's mother, the supportive ally, joined in, emphasising the importance of resolving these matters before Alia's marriage. After careful consideration, Alia's uncle reluctantly agreed, convinced Alia was fully committed to the arranged marriage.

The flight to Dubai was booked for the following Monday, giving Alia a chance to execute her escape plan. Her uncle, reassured by her recent behaviour, returned her phone, laptop, and passport, unaware that these devices would soon become her tools for freedom. Before the departure, Alia attended a dinner with the groom and his family, where the wedding date was finalised. The room buzzed with excitement and anticipation, oblivious to the storm brewing within Alia's heart. She maintained a facade of contentment, knowing that her true intentions were hidden beneath the surface.

As the days ticked by, Alia could not shake off the lingering fear regarding my change of heart. What if my love for her had faded? What if I had moved on? These doubts gnawed at her, threatening to undermine her resolve. Yet, she drew strength from the memories we shared, the promises made, and the love that had endured the test of time.

Yours,
Siddhartha.

Dear new diary,

Little did she know that I was dying to be with her. Little did she know that I would have waited for her till eternity. Only I could tell her what she meant to me. I have such a connection with her soul that I do not think I could have ever moved on with anyone else. Because, Alia is the home I always wanted to return to.

Yours,
Siddhartha.

29th May, 2022

Dear new diary,

As the day of their departure approached, Alia's heart pounded with excitement and trepidation. The Sunday evening was spent packing for the supposedly short trip to Dubai, with Alia carefully concealing her true intentions. Despite the anticipation, she managed to maintain a facade of normalcy, engaging in conversations about wedding arrangements and even discussing makeup salons with the family.

However, Alia was grappling with a wave of emotions beneath the surface. The prospect of leaving her family forever and the life she had known filled her with sadness and uncertainty. She wondered how her uncle would react to her escape and its consequences on her mother and sister. Yet, amidst these doubts, Alia's determination to be with me remained unwavering.

They arrived at the airport early Monday morning, where Alia's uncle bid them farewell with blessings for a safe journey. Alia felt liberated as they boarded the plane to Dubai, knowing that she was one step closer to her goal.

In Dubai, Alia spent the little time she had in clearing her belongings from the hotel and resigning from her job. She constantly maintained the charade of returning to Jordan, informing her uncle of their whereabouts through video calls.

However, on Tuesday morning, Alia took the fateful step towards her new life.

Booking a taxi, Alia and her companions headed to the airport. The journey was filled with an unspoken understanding, each aware of the impending separation and the risks involved. Alia's mother and sister offered encouragement, reminding her of the love and support that would always be with her.

As they reached the airport, Alia hugged her mother and sister tightly, tears streaming down their faces. They exchanged last glances before Alia disappeared into the crowd, her heart pounding with fear and anticipation.

Alia boarded the plane to Los Angeles, the next leg of her journey to freedom and reunion. The 15-hour flight was a period of intense reflection and anticipation. Alia remained in limited contact with her sister and her mother, seeking whatever little comfort and reassurance she could during those long hours.

Meanwhile, Alia's mother and sister continued to play their part, maintaining the illusion that Alia was still with them until she safely reached Los Angeles. They knew that their actions could have severe consequences, but their love for Alia outweighed their fears.

Alia's journey to the United States was a whirlwind of emotions, filled with anticipation, anxiety, and unwavering hope. As the plane soared, her mind raced with questions and doubts.

"What if he's changed?" she wondered, her heart pounding. "How will he react to my sudden reappearance?" The uncertainty gnawed at her, threatening to unravel her carefully constructed plan.

Yet, amidst these fears, Alia's love for me shone like a beacon, guiding her through the darkness. She clung to the memories we shared, our promises, and the bond that had defied distance and time.

The 15-hour long flight stretched like an eternity, each minute testing Alia's patience and resolve. She found solace in the occasional messages from her sister and her mother, their words of encouragement fuelling her determination.

Alia's heart leaped with joy as the plane descended towards Los Angeles. She had finally reached her destination, the land of new beginnings and the promise of reunion. But the final hurdle lay ahead—USA immigration.

With a prayer on her lips and a mix of fear and anticipation coursing through her veins, Alia approached the immigration counter. The officer's questions seemed to echo in her ears, each a potential roadblock to her dreams.

But Alia's unwavering spirit carried her through. She answered each question with a calmness that belied her inner turmoil, focusing solely on the goal that awaited her. And when the officer finally stamped her passport and uttered the words, "Welcome to the USA," Alia's heart soared like a bird set free.

Eager to connect with her mother and sister, Alia found a Wi-Fi hotspot and initiated a video call. Tears streamed down their faces as they shared their happiness and relief, their voices filled with emotion and gratitude.

With a heavy heart, Alia bid farewell to her mother and sister, knowing that their sacrifice would forever be etched in her memory. She promised to make them proud, and to live a life worthy of their love and support.

After the emotional call, Alia wasted no time securing a taxi and heading to USC, her heart pounding with anticipation. The campus was vast and unfamiliar, but she was determined to find me amidst the sea of students.

As fate would have it, Alia encountered an Indian couple, my classmates, who recognised her from my social media posts. She went to the library with their guidance, where she knew I usually spent countless hours preparing for my case studies.

And there, amidst the stacks of books and the hushed whispers of fellow students, Alia found me engaged in a conversation with Alexandria. Her world seemed to come to a standstill as if time had paused to witness this momentous reunion.

All the doubts, fears, and uncertainties melted away in that moment, replaced by an overwhelming surge of love and joy. Alia had finally reached her destination physically, emotionally, and spiritually.

I laid my eyes on you
and I knew that I wanted you
for the rest of my life.

(Alia)

Yours,
Siddhartha.

29th May, 2022

Dear new diary,

Today I was full of overwhelming emotions, as love conquered all. I brought Alia to my humble abode, a place that would soon become our haven, our sanctuary. The excitement of having her under the same roof was palpable, yet anxiety lingered in the air. Alia's heart pounded like a drum as she dialled her mother's number. The phone rang, and in an instant, her mother's voice filled the room, a voice tinged with worry and longing. Tears welled up in Alia's eyes as she saw her mother's face on the screen, a face etched with love and concern.

I watched Alia as she spoke to her mother, every expression of hers mirroring the depth of her emotions. Her voice trembled as she recounted her journey, her hardships, and the unwavering love that guided her to me.

I felt a surge of gratitude towards Alia's mother and sister, two women who had risked everything for their daughter and sister's happiness. Their selfless love was a beacon of light in a world that often seemed consumed by darkness. I vowed to repay their kindness, to cherish their daughter, and to make sure they knew how much their sacrifice meant to us.

As the conversation ended, I took the phone from Alia's trembling hands. I looked into Alia's mother's eyes, which reflected a lifetime of love and sacrifice. I spoke with sincerity and conviction, promising to protect her daughter, to make her happy, and never to let her down.

I also spoke to Alia's sister, her confidante, and her partner in crime. Her joy was infectious, her happiness radiating through the screen. She told Alia of their fabricated story, a tale designed to appease their concerned uncle.

Alia's uncle, a man bound by tradition and duty, was understandably upset. He had trusted Alia, and her disappearance had shaken him. Yet, deep down, he knew Alia's mother and sister were innocent, and that their love for their her was unquestionable.

As the call ended, Alia and I were left in the quiet solitude of our new home. The day's emotions washed over us—a mix of relief, joy, and apprehension. We knew that the road ahead would not be without its challenges, but we also knew that we had love on our side, a love that had defied boundaries and overcome obstacles.

Yours,
Siddhartha.

Finally, we have a world
that is not black and white,
finally, a world
where everyone knows
you are just mine.

29th May, 2022

Dear new diary,

Today, we took the momentous step of calling my mother to reveal the extraordinary events that had transpired over the past few days. My heart pounded with excitement as I prepared to share Alia's courageous journey, unwavering love, and daring escape from Jordan.

Thankfully, my mother's response was full of relief and heartfelt blessings. Her love for Alia shone through her words, and I felt gratitude towards her. We spent the rest of the day recounting our experiences, filling the gaps in each other's stories.

As I narrated my tale, I confessed to Alia the deep despair that had consumed me when I believed I had lost her forever. I revealed my impulsive decision to abandon my studies and return to Dubai in a desperate attempt to find her. However, as fate intervened, Alia's unexpected reappearance rekindled my hope and filled me with overwhelming joy.

Alia, with her gentle understanding, encouraged me to address the lingering situation with Alexandria. I recognised the need for closure, for both her sake and mine. Gathering courage, I approached Alexandria, ready to face the complexities of our past entanglement.

The conversation was difficult, but I found the strength to be honest and transparent. I explained the whirlwind of emotions that had swept me off my feet, the profound impact Alia's presence had on my heart, and the decision we had made to embark on a new chapter together.

To my surprise, Alexandria responded with grace and understanding. She expressed genuine happiness for us, accepting the circumstances with maturity and a remarkable lack of resentment. Her reaction was a testament to her character, and I felt a newfound respect for her.

With the past laid to rest, Alia and I turned our attention to the future, eager to shape our lives together. With my MBA still a year and a half away, we decided I would seek part-time employment to provide financial support, ensuring Alia's well-being as she remained on a tourist visa.

Our hearts overflowed with excitement as we discussed our plans for a wedding—a celebration of our love and commitment. Despite the unconventional path that had led us here, we were grateful for the journey and the unwavering love that had guided us through it all.

Till next time,
Siddhartha.

I feel like
I know you from some other life
Because whatever is happening,
I cannot explain otherwise.

We met in this life
where our souls collided
at the imperfect time
and then we fought
against destiny,
against life,
against death,
against everything that
was keeping us distant,
as if loving each other
was a crime.

30th May, 2022

Dearest new diary,

My heart swells with joy as I pen these words, for today, I celebrate a love that has transcended boundaries and defied all odds. Today, I stand beside my beloved Alia, my wife, my soulmate, the woman who has captured my heart and painted my world with hues of love and happiness.

Our journey has been a tapestry woven with threads of courage, determination, and an unwavering faith in the power of love. Alia, my heart's compass, braved the storms of societal expectations and familial constraints to find her way back into my life. Her love, a beacon of light amidst the darkness, guided me through the shadows of despair and rekindled the flame of hope within me.

Today, we stand united in love, ready to face the world with open arms. With each passing moment, our bond strengthens, our love deepens, and our dreams intertwine. I vow to cherish Alia with every fibre of my being, to stand by her side through life's triumphs and tribulations, and to love her unconditionally, even in the face of adversity.

I will be her pillar of strength, confidant, protector, and her unwavering supporter. I will lift her spirits when clouds of doubt gather, and I will celebrate her every victory with a heart full of

pride. Together, we will navigate the uncharted waters of life, hand in hand, with our love as our guiding light.

I promise to make Alia smile every day, to fill her life with joy and laughter, and to create memories that will forever be etched in our hearts. I will make her feel cherished, valued, and loved beyond measure, ensuring she never regrets her courageous steps to reunite us.

With each passing day, our story unfolds a testament to the power of love to overcome all obstacles. As we embark on this new chapter of our lives together, I can only imagine the beautiful tapestry that love will weave into our future.

Maybe one day, Alia's extended family will understand the depth of our love. Maybe one day, Alia will be able to go back to Jordan to meet her mother and sister. But till then, I will love her even more on the darkest days, so she never regrets why she left everything for me.

Alia's husband,
Siddhartha.

A promise has been made
for all the lives
that we would see.
I will be there to love you
even more
on your darkest days
and kiss you
when you would want
me to go away,
because I love you more than
anyone has ever loved someone
in this universe
and we do belong together
across all the spheres in this world.

The Present

5

I am sitting in our cozy apartment, and my eyes widen as I see her. Alia, my wife, is sitting next to me. She is glowing radiantly, with a beauty that always takes my breath away. She is wearing a traditional red Indian saree and has a few bangles on her wrists. She has applied a bindi on her forehead and kept her hair down. Every time she shakes her head, her hair falls on her face, and like always, I push them back. And, Alia smiles every time I do that.

Excited over our new beginnings, a surge of pride fills my chest as I recall our journey together. I wrap my arm around her and tease, "So, tell me again, why did you leave everything and come to this country for me?"

She laughs softly and rests her head on my shoulder. "Because I love you, silly. And because I wanted to see the world with you."

I kiss her forehead and smile. "And are you glad you did that?"

She nods and looks into my eyes. "Yes, I am. But..."

She hesitates and bites her lip. I sense something is wrong. "But what, honey? What is the matter?"

She leans in and softly presses her lips to my ear, "I took this step because I wondered—What if there is no tomorrow?"

At that moment, I felt that my life had come full circle.

Acknowledgement

I have been writing poems for many years now. After the love my first novel received from people across the globe, I was encouraged to expand my horizons and write an even lengthier love story in a unique format, combining both prose and poetry.

I would not have completed this book without the support of two important people—my mother and my partner. My mother has been the guiding light throughout my life and has constantly motivated me to take up writing. My partner has always inspired me to go beyond my comfort zone and follow my passions. With their sheer support and encouragement, I was able to follow my dreams along with my full-time job.

I would also like to thank my Artwork Designer, Fatema, who breathed life into the words through her art.

Then, my dearest friend Alaa, who proofread my book, listened to all my poems and provided valuable feedback to help me become a better author.

Last but not the least, my soul friend Seema, who encouraged me to open up a poetry page to share my words with the world. And the page actually proved to be the stepping stone for my entire writing journey till now.

Thank you, everyone!

About the Author

Shuchi Batra is a poet and novelist from India. She has been writing poems since she was 8 years old and has a dedicated poetry page on Instagram with over 85k followers. She has written more than a thousand micro poems to date and believes that words not only express emotions but also provide relief from pain, helping one move on from undesirable life situations.

Her first novel, 'A Million Times Over' is a unique love story told in the form of poems. It was published in 2021 and became an Amazon bestseller. The novel also received positive reviews from national newspapers, magazines, and social media influencers.

Shuchi aims to become India's bestselling author with her innovative and expressive writing style. She is a banker by profession and an MBA graduate from the Indian Institute of Management, Indore. She is currently settled in the USA with her husband.

About the Author